'STORY OF O – notorious as an underground novel, remarkable as a rare instance of pornography sublimed to purest art – appeared first under mysterious circumstances at Paris in 1954 . . . STORY OF O is neither a fantasy nor a case history. With its alternate beginnings and endings; its simple direct style (like that of a fable); its curious air of abstraction, of independence from time, place and personality, what it resembles most is a legend – the spiritual history of a saint and martyr. . . . Commencing with the simplest of situations, the story gradually opens out into a Daedalian maze of perverse relationships – a clandestine society of sinister formality and elegance where the primary bond is mutual complicity in dedication to the pleasures of sadism and masochism. . . .' – *New York Times Book Review*

'A remarkable piece of work' – *Harold Pinter*

'I do believe that Pauline Réage has confounded all her critics and made pornography (if that is what it is) an art' – *Brian Aldiss*

Pauline Réage
Story of O

With an essay by Jean Paulhan
of the Académie Française

CORGI BOOKS
A DIVISION OF TRANSWORLD PUBLISHERS LTD

STORY OF O
A CORGI BOOK 0 552 10167 2

Originally published in Great Britain by
The Olympia Press (England) Ltd.

PRINTING HISTORY
Olympia Press edition published 1970
Corgi edition published 1972
Corgi edition reprinted 1973
Corgi edition reprinted 1975
Corgi edition reissued 1976
Corgi edition reprinted 1976
Corgi edition reprinted 1977
Corgi edition reprinted 1978
Corgi edition reprinted 1979
Corgi edition reprinted 1980 (twice)

This book is set in 10 on 11 point Intertype Plantin

Corgi Books are published by Transworld Publishers Ltd.,
Century House, 61–63 Uxbridge Road,
Ealing, London W5 5SA.
Made and printed in Great Britain by
Hunt Barnard Printing Ltd., Aylesbury, Bucks.

I

THE LOVERS OF ROISSY

Her lover one day takes O for a walk, but this time in a part of the city – the Parc Montsouris, the Parc Monceau – where they've never been together before. After they've strolled awhile along the paths, after they've sat down side by side on a bench near the grass, and got up again, and moved on towards the edge of the park, there, where two streets meet, where there never used to be any taxi-stand, they see a car, at that corner. It looks like a taxi, for it does have a meter. 'Get in,' he says; she gets in. It's late in the afternoon, it's autumn. She is wearing what she always wears: high heels, a suit with a pleated skirt, a silk blouse, no hat. But she has on long gloves reaching up to the sleeves of her jacket, in her leather handbag she's got her papers, and her compact and lipstick. The taxi eases off, very slowly; nor has the man next to her said a word to the driver. But on the right, on the left, he draws down the little window-shades, and the one behind too; thinking that he is about to kiss her, or so as to caress him, she has slipped off her gloves. Instead, he says: 'I'll take your bag, it's in your way.' She give it to him, he puts it beyond her reach; then adds: 'You've too much clothing on. Unhitch your stockings, roll them down to just above your knees. Go ahead,' and he gives her some elastics to hold the stockings in place. It isn't easy, not in the car, which is going faster now, and she doesn't want to have the driver turn around. But she manages anyhow, at last; it's a queer, uncomfortable feeling, the contact of silk of her slip upon her naked and free legs, and the unattached garters are sliding loosely back and forth across her

5

skin. 'Undo your garter-belt,' he says, 'take off your panties.'
There's nothing to that, all she has to do is get at the hook behind and raise up a little. He takes the garter-belt from her
hand, he takes the panties, opens her bag, puts them away inside
it; then he says: 'You're not to sit on your slip or on your skirt,
pull them up and sit on the seat without anything in between.'
The seat-covering is a sort of leather, slick and chilly; it's a
very strange sensation, the way it sticks and clings to her
thighs. Then he says: 'Now put your gloves back on.' The taxi
goes right along and she doesn't dare ask why René is so quiet,
so still, or what all this means to him: she so motionless and so
silent, so denuded and so offered, though so thoroughly gloved,
in a black car going she hasn't the least idea where. He hasn't
told her to do anything or not to do it, but she doesn't dare
either cross her legs or sit with them held together. One on this
side, one on that side, she rests her gloved hands on the seat,
pushing down.

'Here we are,' he says all of a sudden. Here we are: the taxi
comes to a stop on a fine avenue, under a tree – those are plane
trees – in front of a small mansion, you could just see it, nestled
away between courtyard and garden, the way the Faubourg
Saint-Germain mansions are. There's no streetlight nearby, it
is dark inside the cab, and outside rain is falling. 'Don't move,'
says René. 'Don't move a muscle.' He extends his hand towards the neck of her blouse, unties the ribbon at the throat,
then unbuttons the buttons. She leans forward ever so little,
and believes he is about to caress her breasts. But no; he's got
a small penknife out, he's only groping for the shoulder-straps
of her brassiere, he cuts the straps, removes the brassiere. He
has closed her blouse again and now, underneath, her breasts
are free and nude, like her belly and thighs are nude and free,
like all of her is, from waist to knee.

'Listen,' he says. 'You're ready. Here's where I leave you.
You're going to get out and go to the door and ring the bell.
Someone will open the door, whoever it is you'll do as he says.
You'll do it right away and willingly of your own accord, else
they'll make you, if you don't obey at once, they'll make you
obey. What? No, you don't need your bag any more. You don't

6

need anything, you're just the whore, I'm the pimp who's furnishing you. Yes, certainly, I'll be there, sure. Now go.'

Another version of the same beginning was simpler, more direct: similarly dressed, the young woman was taken off in a car by her lover and by a second man, an unknown friend of his. The stranger drove, the lover was seated beside the young woman; and the one who did the talking, the friend, the unknown stranger in front, explained to the young woman that her lover's task was to prepare her, that he was now going to tie her hands behind her back, unfasten her stockings and roll them down, remove her garter-belt, her panties, her brassiere, and blindfold her; that afterwards she would be taken to the château where she would receive instructions in due course, as events required. And so indeed it had been: once undressed and bound in this manner, and after about a thirty minutes' drive, she was helped out of the car and marched a few steps. Still blindfolded, she passed one or two doors and then found herself alone, the blindfold gone, standing in a darkened room where she was left for half an hour, for an hour, for two – I don't know, but it seemed as though it were an age. When the door finally opened and the light was turned on, you could see that she'd been waiting in a room, just a room, comfortable, yet odd. There was a thick carpet on the floor, but not a stick of furniture in that room. The walls were lined with cupboards. Two girls opened the door – two pretty young women costumed like eighteenth-century chambermaids, with long, light, puffy skirts that came to the floor, tight bodices that made the bust rise and swell and that were laced or hooked in back, gauze kerchiefs at the neck, wearing elbow-length gauze gloves to match. Their eyes and mouths were painted. Each wore a collar around her neck and bracelets on her wrists.

And then I know that they released O's hands, until that point still tied behind her back, and told her to undress. They were going to bathe her and make her up. But they made her stand still; they did everything for her, they stripped her and laid her clothes neatly away in one of the cupboards. They did not let her do her own bathing, they washed her themselves and set her hair just as hairdressers would have, making her sit in one of those big chairs that tilt backwards when your hair is being washed and then come up again when the drier is applied. That took at least an hour. She was seated nude in the chair and they prohibited her from either crossing her legs or pressing them together. As, on the opposite wall, there was a mirror running from floor to ceiling and straight ahead of her, in plain view, every time she glanced up she caught sight of herself, of her open body.

When she was made up, her eyelids lightly shadowed, her mouth very red, the point and halo of her nipples rouged, the sides of the lips of her sex reddened, a lingering scent applied to the fur of her armpits and her pubis, to the crease between her buttocks, to beneath her breasts and the palms of her hands, she was led into a room where a threesided mirror and, facing it, a fourth mirror on the opposite wall enabled, indeed obliged, her to see her own image reflected. She was told to sit on a hassock placed between the mirrors, and to wait. The hassock was upholstered with prickly black fur; the rug was black, the walls red. She wore red slippers. Set in one of the little boudoir's walls was a casement window giving out upon a magnificent but sombre, formal garden. The rain had stopped and the trees were swaying in the wind while the moon raced high among the clouds. I don't know just how long she remained in the red boudoir, nor if she really was alone, as she thought she was, for someone may perhaps have been watching her through a peephole disguised somewhere in the wall. What I do know is that when the two chambermaids returned, one was carrying a tape-measure and the other had a basket over her arm. With them came a man wearing a trailing violet robe with sleeves cut wide at the shoulder and gathered in at the wrist; as he walked, the robe showed to be open at the waist. You could make out that he was in some kind of tights which covered his legs and thighs but left his sex free. It was the sex that O saw first, then the whip made of strands of leather, the whip was stuck in his belt, then she noticed that the man was masked in a black hood completed by a section of black gauze hiding his eyes – and finally she noticed the fine black kid-gloves he was

8

wearing. He ordered her not to move, he told the women to hurry. The one with the tape took the measure of O's neck and wrists. Although somewhat small, her sizes were in no way out of the ordinary, and they had no trouble selecting a suitable collar and bracelets from the assortment contained in the basket. Both collar and bracelets were fashioned of many layers of thin leather, the whole being no thicker than a finger, fitted with a catch that worked automatically, like a padlock, and which needed a key to be opened. Next to the catch, and imbedded in the leather, was a metal ring. They fitted snugly, but not so tightly as to chafe or break the skin. After they had been set in place, the man told her to rise. He himself sat on the fur-covered hassock and made her approach until she stood against his knees. He passed his gloved hand between her thighs and over her breast and explained to her that she would be presented that same evening after she had dined. Still nude, she took her meal alone in a kind of small cabin; an unseen hand passed the plates to her through a little window. When she had finished eating, the two maids came for her again. In the boudoir, they had her put her hands behind her back and secured them there by means of the rings of her wristbands; they draped a long red cape over her shoulders, and it was fastened to the ring set in her collar. The cape covered her completely, but with her hands behind her back that way she couldn't prevent it from opening when she walked. One woman preceded her, and opened the doors; the second followed, and shut them again. They filed through a vestibule, through two drawing-rooms, and entered the library where four men were at coffee. They wore the same flowing robes as the first she had seen, but were not masked. Nevertheless, O did not have time to observe their faces or recognize whether her lover was there (he was), for one of the men trained a spotlight upon her face, dazzling her. Everyone stood in silence, the women on either side, the men in front, watching her. Then the light was switched off and the women went away, but a blindfold had been placed over O's eyes. Stumbling a bit, she was made to advance and could sense that she was standing before the fire around which the four men had been grouped. In the quiet, she could hear

9

the soft crackling of the logs and feel the heat; she was facing the fire. Two hands lifted away her cape, two others checked the clasp on her wristbands and descended inspectingly down over her buttocks. These hands were not gloved, and one of them simultaneously penetrated her in two places – so brusquely that she let out a cry. Some voice laughed. Another said: 'Turn her around so we can see her breasts and belly.' She was turned about, and now it was on her buttocks that she felt the glow of the fire. A hand moulded itself round one of her breasts, squeezed, a mouth closed upon the nipple of her other breast. Suddenly, she lost her balance and tottered backwards into unknown arms. At the same instant, her legs were spread apart and her lips gently worked open – hair grazed the inner surfaces of her thighs. She heard a voice declare that she ought to be made to kneel, and she was. It was painful to be on her knees, seated on her heels in the position nuns take when they pray.

'You've never imposed physical restraints, for example tied her up?'

'No, never.'

'Or whipped her?'

'Never. Though, the fact is –' It was her lover who was answering.

'The fact is,' said the other voice, 'that if you do tie her up, if you use a whip on her, and if she likes that – then no, you understand. Pleasure, we've got to move beyond that stage. We must make the tears flow.'

She was then drawn to her feet, and they were probably about to detach her hands so as to tie her to some post or other or to the wall, when someone interrupted, saying that before anything else he wanted her – immediately. She was forced down upon her knees again, but this time a hassock was placed as a support under her chest; her hands were still fixed behind her back, her haunches were higher than her torso. One of the men gripped her buttocks and sank himself into her womb. When he was done, he ceded his place to a second. The third wanted to drive his way into the narrower passage and, pushing hard, violently, wrung a scream from her lips. When at last he let go of her, moaning and tears streaming down under her blindfold, she slipped sidewise to the floor only to discover by the pressure of two knees against her face that her mouth was not to be spared either. Finally, finished with her, they moved off, leaving her, a captive in her finery, huddled, collapsed on the carpet before the fire. She heard drink being poured, glasses tinkling, chairs stirring; logs were added to the fire. Then her blindfold was suddenly snatched away. It was a large room. Bookcases lined the walls, dimly lit by a bracketed lamp and the flicker of the fire. Two of the men were standing; they were smoking. Another was seated, a riding crop across his knees, and there was still another leaning over her, caressing her breasts; that one was her lover. All four had taken her and she had not been able to distinguish him from amongst the rest.

It was explained to her that as long as she was in this château it would always be this way: she would see the faces of those who violated and bullied her, but never at night, and in this way she would never know which ones were responsible for the worst of her sufferings. When she was whipped the same would hold true, except when it was desired that she see herself being whipped, as happened to be the case this first time: no blindfold, but the men in masks in order to be unidentifiable. Her lover had picked her up and set her, in her red cape, on the arm of a large chair in the corner by the chimney, so that she might listen to what they had to tell her and see what they wished to exhibit to her. Her hands were still pinioned behind her back. She was shown the riding-crop, black, long and slender, made of fine bamboo sheathed in leather, an article such as one finds in the display-windows of expensive saddle-makers' shops; the leather whip – the one she'd seen tucked in the first man's belt – was long, with six lashes each ending in a knot; there was a third whip whose numerous light cords were several times knotted and stiff, quite as if soaked in water, and they actually had been soaked in water, as O was able to verify when they stroked her belly with those cords and, opening her thighs, exposing her hidden parts, let the damp, cold ends trail against the tender membranes. On the console there

11

yet remained the collection of keys and the steel chains. Midway up one of the library's walls ran a balcony supported by two pillars. In one of these, as high up as a man standing on tip-toe could reach, was sunk a hook. O, whose lover had taken her in his arms, one hand under her shoulder, the other in her womb which was burning her almost unbearably, O was informed that when, as soon they would, they unfastened her hands, it would only be to attach them to this whipping-post by means of those bracelets on her wrists and this steel chain. With the exception of her hands, which would be immobilized a little above her head, she would be able to move, to turn, to face around and see the strokes coming, they told her; by and large, they'd confine the whipping to her buttocks and thighs, to the space, that is to say, between her waist and her knees, precisely that part of her which had been prepared in the car when she had been made to sit naked on the seat; it was likely, however, that some one of the four men would want to score her with the crop, for it caused fine, long, deep welts which lasted quite some time. They'd go about it gradually, giving her ample opportunity to scream and fight and cry to her heart's content. They'd pause to let her catch her breath, but after she'd recovered it, they'd start in again, judging the results not by her screams or her tears but by the more or less livid and durable marks traced in her flesh by the whips. It was called to her attention that these criteria for estimating the effectiveness of the whip, apart from their just impartiality and from the fact they rendered unnecessary any attempts victims might make to elicit pity by exaggerating their moans, did not by any means bar open-air whipping – there would indeed be a good deal of that in the park outside the château – or for that matter, whipping in any ordinary apartment or hotel room provided a tight gag were employed (they showed her a gag), which, while giving free rein to tears, stifles any scream and even makes moaning difficult.

They did not, however, intend to use the gag that night. To the contrary, they were eager to hear O howl, the sooner the better. Proud, she steeled herself to resist, she gritted her teeth; but not for long. They soon heard her beg to be let loose, beg them to stop, stop for a second, for just one second. So frantically did she twist and wheel to dodge the biting lashes that she almost spun in circles. The chain, although unyielding, for, after all, it was a chain, was nevertheless slack enough to allow her leeway. Owing to her excessive writhing, her belly and the front of her thighs received almost as heavy a share as her rear. They left off for a moment, deeming it better to tie her flat up against the post by means of a rope passed around her waist; the rope being cinched tight, her head necessarily angled to one side of the post and her flanks jutted to the other, thereby placing her rump in a prominent position. From then on, every deliberately aimed blow dealt her struck home. In view of the manner in which her lover had exposed her to this, O might well have supposed that an appeal to his pity would have been the surest way to increase his cruelty, so great was his pleasure in wresting or in having the others wrest these from her decisive proofs of his power over her. And it was in fact he who was the first to observe that the leather whip, with which they'd begun marked her the least (for the moistened lash had obtained strong results almost instantly, and the crop with the first blow struck), and hence, by employing no other, they could prolong the ordeal and, after brief pauses, start in again just about immediately or according to their fancy. He asked that they use only that first whip. Meanwhile, the man who liked women only for what they had in common with men, seduced by the sight of that proffered behind straining out from under the taut rope and made all the more tempting by its wrigglings to escape, requested an intermission in order to take advantage of it; he spread apart the two burning halves and penetrated, but not without difficulty, which brought him to remark that they'd have to contrive to make this thoroughfare easier of access. The thing could be done, they agreed, and decided that the proper measures would be taken.

The young woman, swaying and half fainting under her flowing red cape, was released then and, before being led away to the cell where she was to stay, they had her sit down in a chair by the fireside and listen while there were outlined to her, in detail, all the rules she was to observe during her period at the château and also during her everyday life once she'd returned home from the château (not, however, that she was going to recover her former freedom); one of the men rang. The two costumed maids who had received her now appeared, bringing the clothes she was to wear and tokens whereby those who had been guests at the château prior to her coming and after it might be able to recognize her when later on she had left. This costume was similar to the chambermaids'. Over a whalebone bodice which severely constricted the waist, and over a starched linen petticoat, was worn an ample gown, the open neck of which left the breasts, raised by the bodice, practically visible beneath a light film of gauze. The petticoat and gauze were white, the bodice and gown a seagreen satin. When O was dressed and reseated beside the fireplace, her pallor intensified by the paleness of the gown, the two girls, who had not uttered a word, made ready to leave. As they were going, one of the men stepped forward, signalled to her nearest the door to wait, and brought the other back towards O. He took her by the waist with one hand and raised her skirts with the other, making her turn, displaying the costume's practical advantages, having O admire its design, and explaining that, simply by means of a belt, the skirts could be held at any desired height, thus, which meant that all of what was exposed was very ready to hand, thus. As a matter of fact, he added, they often had the girls stroll in the garden or move about the château with their skirts hitched up behind, or – thus – hitched up in front, at the level of the midriff. He bade the girl demonstrate to O how the skirt was to be kept in the right position: how she was to take in the folds, roll them (like a lock of hair in a curler), keep them just so by means of a belt, the buckle exactly in front, so as to leave the way clear to the womb, or this other way, so, in back to expose the buttocks. In both instances, petticoat and skirt were to fall away in flowing diagonal folds. Like O, the girl's flanks bore fresh marks of the riding-crop. She went away.

This is the speech they then made to O:

'You are here to serve your masters. During the day, in connection with the maintenance of the household, you will perform whatever chores are assigned to you, such as sweeping, putting the books back in place, arranging flowers, or waiting upon table. Your tasks will not be more onerous than these. But at the first word or gesture you will stop in the middle of whatever you happen to be doing, addressing yourself to your one primary task, your only significant one duty, which is to avail yourself to be used. Your hands are not your own, neither are your breasts, nor, above all, is any one of the orifices of your body, which we are at liberty to explore and into which we may, whenever we so please, introduce ourselves. In order that you bear it constantly, or as constantly as possible, in mind that you have lost the right to withhold or deny yourself, in our presence you will at all times avoid altogether closing your labia, nor will you ever cross your legs, nor press your knees together (as, you recall, was forbidden to you directly you set out for this place), which will signify, in your view and in ours, that your mouth, your belly and your behind are constantly at our entire disposal. Before us, you must never touch your breasts: your bodice lifts them supplicatingly to us, they are ours. During the day, since you will be dressed, you will raise your skirt if ordered to, and whoever would have you will use you as he likes, undisguised; but he will not whip you. The whip will only be applied between the hours of sundown and dawn. But over and above those whippings, which you will receive from whoever desires to whip you, you will be punished, in the form of further whipping, at night for any infraction of the rules during the day: that is to say, for thoughtlessness, for insubmissiveness, for having raised your eyes upon whoever speaks to or takes you: never must you look any one of us in the face. If our night-time costume, what we are wearing now, leaves our sex uncovered, it is not for the sake of convenience, since it would be just as convenient otherwise, but for that of insolence, so that your eyes will focus themselves there and nowhere else, so that you will come finally to understand that there resides your master, your lord, to whom all of you is destined and above all your lips. In the day, when we are dressed in the usual manner and you as you are now, you will observe the same rule and when requested you will simply open

15

our clothing and later close it again when we are finished with you. Also, at night, you will have only your lips wherewith to do us honour, and also your widespread thighs, since, at night, you will have your hands secured behind your back and you will be nude, as you were when brought here a short while ago; you will not be blindfolded save when you are to be maltreated and, now that you have seen yourself being beaten, when you are whipped. In this regard, if it were advisable that you accustom yourself to whipping – and it shall be frequent, daily, so long as you remain here – it is less for our pleasure than for your instruction. This may be stressed by the fact that, on those nights when no one wants you, you may expect a visit from the valet who has been appointed to the job: he will enter your cell and, in the solitude, mete out to you what you need to receive and which we are not inclined to bestow. Actually, the object of these procedures, as well as of the chain which will be affixed to your collar, is to confine you to within a limited scope and more or less to your bed for several hours every day, a good deal less to make you suffer pain, scream or shed tears than, by means of this pain, to enforce upon you the idea that you are subject to constraint and to teach you that you utterly belong to something which is apart from and outside yourself. When you are dismissed from here, you will go forth wearing an iron ring on your finger; by it others will recognize you. You will then have learned to obey those who wear the same token – upon seeing it, they will know that you are constantly naked beneath your skirt, however correct or ordinary your dress and that this in their behalf, this nudity for them. Those who find you unco-operative will bring you back here. You will now be shown to your cell.'

While these words were being uttered to O, the two women who had come to dress her were standing the whole while on either side of the post where she had been whipped; but they avoided touching it, as though it frightened them or (which was more likely) as though they had been forbidden to touch it; when the man had concluded, they moved towards O, who understood that she was to rise and follow them. And so she got to her feet, collecting her skirts to keep from stumbling, for she wasn't used to long dresses, nor to managing in these thick-soled and very high-heeled clogs which only a single broad band of satin, of the same green as her gown, prevented from slipping off. Stooping to gather her skirts, she cast a quick glance around. The women were waiting, the men had shifted their attention elsewhere. Her lover, sitting on the floor, his back propped against the hassock over which she'd been bent earlier in the evening, his legs drawn up and his elbows resting on his knees, was idly toying with the leather whip. At the first step she took to overtake the women, the edge of her skirt brushed him and he looked up, smiling; he pronounced her name, also rose to his feet. Gently, he caressed her hair, ran the tip of his finger gently along her eyebrows, gently kissed her lips. He gazed at her and, aloud, said that he loved her. Trembling, O was terrified to hear herself say: 'I love you,' and it was true, she did. He pressed her to him and said: 'My love, my darling,' then kissed her chin, kissed her neck, kissed the corner of her cheek, for she had let her head sink upon the shoulder of his violet robe. Murmuring now, he repeated that he loved her and, murmuring still, he said: 'Now kneel down, caress me, kiss me.' He backed a step away from her, motioning the women back and leaning an elbow upon the console. He was tall, but the console was not very high, and his long legs, sheathed in the same violet as her dress, were slightly bent at the knees over which the open robe hung like a drapery. The top of the console, pushing against his buttocks from behind, thrust forward the heavy sex and the light fleece that crowned it. The three men drew near. O knelt on the rug, her green skirt spreading round her in a pool, her bodice holding her breasts, the nipples visible, at the level of her lover's knees. 'A little more light,' said one of the men. As they were directing the beam so that it would fall upon his sex and upon the face of his mistress, who was completely ready, and upon her hands, which were already caressing him, René said: 'Say it once again. Say "I love you."' O said: 'I love you,' said it with such delight that she scarcely dared touch her lips to the tip of his sex, still protected by its mantlet of soft skin. The three men were smoking, commenting upon her movements, upon the way her mouth closed over and worked at the sex it had seized and along whose length it ran, ran back and forth, upon how tears came to her eyes every time the swollen member struck the back of her throat, causing her to choke, to shudder as though from an imminent nausea. It was with her mouth still half-gagged by the hardened flesh filling it that she brought out, again, thickly, the words: 'I love you.' The two women had stationed themselves one on either side of René who, leaning his hands on their shoulders, had lowered himself towards O. She heard the remarks being made by the witnesses, but listened through them for her lover's moans, caressing him carefully, with infinite respect and slowly, in the way she knew he liked. O was aware of the splendour of her mouth, of its beauty, since her lover deigned to enter it, since he deigned to make a spectacle of its caresses, since he deigned to shed his seed in it. She received him as one receives a god, with thanksgiving heard his cry, joyously heard the others laugh, and when once she had received him, fell, unstrung, and lay with her face against the floor. The two women aided her to rise, and this time led her away.

The clogs clacked upon the red tiles of those hallways; they passed door after door: discreet, tidy all these doors had tiny keyholes, tiny locks, like the doors to rooms in the best hotels. O was working up courage to ask whether these rooms were all inhabited, and by whom, when one of her companions, whose voice she had not hitherto heard, told her: 'You are in the red wing. Your valet's name is Pierre.'

'What valet?' O asked, impressed by the gentleness of that voice. 'And what is your name?'

'Andrée.'

'I'm Jeanne,' said the second.

The first continued: 'The valet has the keys, it is he who will chain you and unchain you, who will whip you when you are to be punished and when they haven't the time to do it themselves.'

'I was in the red wing last year,' said Jeanne, 'Pierre had arrived by then, he was there. He often came at night; the

18

valets have the keys. They have the right to use those of us who are in their section. Whenever they wish.'

O was preparing to ask what Pierre was like. But she did not have the opportunity: for at that bend in the hallway they halted before a door in no way unlike any of the others. Between this and the next door was a small bench; sitting on it, a kind of peasant, squat, ruddy-faced, his hair close-cropped, nearly shaven, with little deep-set black eyes and rolls of fat at his neck. He was dressed like an operetta valet: in a frill-shirt whose lace collar protruded from a red domestic's jacket under which he had on a black waistcoat. His breeches were black, his stockings white, he had on patent-leather shoes with buckles. He, too, at his belt, carried a many-thonged leather whip. Red hairs covered his hands. He stood, drew a master-key from a pocket in his waistcoat, unlocked the door, ushered the three women in, saying: 'I'm locking, ring when you're done.'

There was hardly anything to the cell, as for size, although it was actually made up of two rooms. With the hall door shut, one found oneself in an antechamber giving into the cell proper; inside it and next to this entry was another door leading to a bathroom. At the far end, as one looked in, was a window. Against the wall to the left, between bathroom door and window, was the headboard of a large squarish bed, quite low and covered with furs. There was no other furniture, no mirror. The walls were done in a bright red, the carpet was black. Andrée had O notice that the bed was less a bed than a mattressed platform covered with a spread made of material that only looked like fur. Flat and hard too, the pillowcase was of the same cloth. The one object to be seen on an otherwise bare wall, at about the same distance above the bed as the hook in the post was above the floor of the library, was a large ring of gleaming steel from which descended a long steel chain, its lower end forming a little pile of links on the bed, finishing in a padlocked catch: the whole thing was like a slender drapery, drawn neatly back and, as though held by a loop, in its stillness it had a clean, cool look of orderliness.

19

'We must have you take your bath,' said Jeanne. 'I'll undo your dress.'

The only noticeable features about the bathroom were the Turkish toilet, set in the corner nearest the door, and the presence of mirrors entirely covering every wall. Andrée and Jeanne did not allow O to enter until she was naked; they laid her dress in the closet next to the washstand where her clogs and red cape had already been put away, and stayed with her so that when she squatted down over the toilet she discovered herself surrounded by as many reflected images, and as equally revealing, as when she had been forced by unknown hands in the library.

'Not now,' said Jeanne. 'Wait till Pierre comes, then you can look.'

'Why wait for Pierre?'

'When he comes to fasten the chain he may perhaps make you squat.'

O sensed herself grow pale. 'But why?' she demanded.

'You'll just have to,' Jeanne replied. 'But you're lucky.'

'Lucky?'

'Your lover brought you here, didn't he?'

'Yes,' O said.

'Then they'll be much harder on you.'

'I don't understand –'

'You will very soon. I'll ring for Pierre. We'll come to get you tomorrow morning.'

Andrée wore a smile as she left; and Jeanne, before following her out, caressed the tips of O's breasts – O, dumbfounded, stood at the foot of the bed. Apart from the leather collar and wristbands, hardened and constricted by the water from her bath, she was nude.

'And here we have the lovely lady,' said the valet as he entered and caught hold of her two hands. He slipped the catch of one wristband into the other, snapped them shut, thus joining the inside of her wrists tightly together; then, raising her hands, he secured them to the catch of her collar. Which left her with her hands, pressed palm to palm, at the level of her neck, as when one prays. All that now remained was to chain her to the wall, and the chain was there in readiness. He unlocked the hasp at the chain's upper end and made some adjustments, shortening it. O was obliged to move closer to the head of the bed, upon which Pierre had her lie down. The chain slid clicking through the ring until at last the young woman could only move to right or left on the bed or stand erect on either side of the headboard. As the chain was pulling the collar round behind and as, at the same time, her hands tended to pull it round to the front, an equilibrium was struck, bringing her joined hands to lie upon her left shoulder towards which her head was also leaning. The valet drew the black coverlet over O, but not until he had first drawn her legs up towards her chest and peered for a moment at the opening between her thighs. After that, he didn't touch her again, didn't say a word; he extinguished the light – the lamp was on the wall between the two doors – and left.

Lying on her left side, and alone in the darkness and the silence, hot between the two layers of fur, O wondered why such a great mildness mingled with the terror within her, or why terror should have such a sweet taste. She became aware that, in large measure, her distress was caused by her inability to use her hands; not that her hands could have protected her (did she indeed really desire to protect herself?), but, her hands free, she would have been able to make a gesture of self-defense, a little gesture, would have made a little attempt to thrust away the hands that had seized her, the flesh that had transpierced her, to shield her flesh from the whip. They had sundered her from hands, freed her of them; her body under the fur, her own body itself was inaccessible to her; how odd it was, not to be able to touch one's own knees, nor the slit of one's own womb. Her lips, the lips between her own legs, which were burning her, were forbidden to her, and perhaps burned her because she knew they were open, awaiting whoever might happen to want them: openly awaiting Pierre, the valet, if he were to choose to enter between them. She was amazed to find that the memory of the whip could leave her so tranquil, so serene; whilst the thought that she would probably

21

never know which of the four men had twice forced himself into her behind, nor know if it had indeed been man who had done it two times, nor know whether it might not have been her lover – this thought overwhelmed her. She slithered up and down on her belly for a moment, thinking that her lover loved the furrow between her buttocks, that he had never before this evening (if it had been he) penetrated her there. She did hope that it had been René; could she ask him? Might she? Ah, no, never. Once again she saw the hand which, in the car, had taken her garter-belt and her panties from her, and held the elastics stretched while she rolled her stockings down to just above the knee. So keen was the image that she forgot her hands were bound, and the chain grated. And why should it be that, if the remembrance of her lashing weighed so lightly upon her, the mere thought, the mere sight of the whip, the very word itself, made her heart beat wildly and made her wince, her eyes tight with terror? She did not stop to consider whether it were only terror; a panic laid hold of her : there'd be a jerk on her chain, it'd be hauled down, she'd be dragged up till she stood on her bed and she'd be whipped, her belly glued against the wall, she'd be whipped, and whipped, and whipped; the word whirled in her brain. Pierre would whip her, Jeanne had told her so. You're lucky, Jeanne had repeated, they'll be much harder on you; what had she meant by that? Then she ceased to be conscious of anything except the collar, the bracelets and the chain; her body began to drift, to vanish in the wake, she was going to understand. And she went to sleep.

In the final hours of the night, when it is darkest, when it is coldest, just before dawn, Pierre reappeared. He switched on the bathroom light, leaving the door to it open; thus, a square of light was thrown upon the centre of the bed where O's body, slender and curled up, made a small mound under the blanket. This Pierre snatched away, in silence. As O was lying on her left side, her face towards the window, her knees somewhat bent, it was her white flanks reclining on black fur that met his gaze. He removed the pillow from under her head; politely, he said: 'Would you please stand,' and when, helping herself

22

by holding onto the chain, she had reached her knees, he took her elbows to aid her the rest of the way up; she faced the wall, her forearms and elbows were flush against it. The illumination cast upon the bed was faint, since the bed was black, and while it made her body visible, his gestures were not. Without being able to see, she guessed he was lessening the length of the chain and refastening it by another link so as to keep her upright; by the pressure on her neck she felt the chain grow taut. Her naked feet rested flat upon the bed. Nor did she see that, at his belt, instead of the leather whip, he was carrying a black crop similar to the one with which she had been struck earlier but struck only twice, and they'd been flicks rather than cuts she'd received at the pillory. Pierre's left hand settled upon her waist, she sensed the mattress give a little, for he had put his right foot upon it to gain purchase, he was bracing himself. And then, at that same moment, O heard a whistle in the gloom, and she felt an atrocious blaze rip across her flanks, and she yelled. Pierre plied the crop with all his might. He did not wait for her screams to subside, and four times over began anew, taking care to deliver the blows either above or below the spot he had been working over previously, so that the pattern of welts would be distinct. Even after Pierre had stopped she went right on screaming, and her tears continued to flow into her open mouth. 'Kindly turn around,' he said; and she, as if smitten, failing to respond, he seized her haunches without letting go of the crop, whose handle grazed her ribs. When he had turned her about-face, he moved off a little; then, with all his force, swung his crop against the front of her thighs. All in all, it had lasted five minutes. When he had gone, after snapping out the light and closing the bathroom door, O, moaning, dangling at the end of the chain, swayed to and fro against the wall, in the darkness. She sought to quiet herself, and lay still against the bright percale covering the wall; the cloth cool against her tortured flesh, she lay still all the while the day sought to break. The long window towards which she was turned, for she was leaning one hip to the wall, looked east; that window extended from floor to ceiling, was uncurtained although framed by the same red material applied adorning the wall and which, in the embrasure, on either side fell in heavy folds. O watched a pale dawn slowly break, the night mists trailing yet upon the clustered asters outside and below the window, the thinning damps finally disclosing a poplar tree. Yellowed leaves sifted down in spirals from time to time, even though there was no wind. From the window, after the banks of mauve asters, a lawn was visible, and beyond its expanse, a walk. And now it was broad daylight that shone, and it had been a long time since O had last stirred. A gardener came along the walk, he was pushing a wheelbarrow. Its iron wheel could be heard crunching on the gravel. Had he come nearer to rake up the leaves fallen by the asters, that window was so large and the room so small and so brightly lit that he'd have seen O, enchained and naked, and the marks the crop had left on her thighs. The welts had swollen and formed narrow ridges of a much darker red than the red of the wall. Where did her lover lie sleeping, as he loved to sleep on calm mornings? In which room, upon what bed? Did he know to what tortures he had delivered her up? Was it he who had prescribed them? O's thoughts turned to those prisoners shown in the engravings that illustrate history books, men who had been chained and whipped too a long, long time ago, centuries ago, and who were dead. She did not want to die; but if torture were the price she was to have to pay for her lover's continuing love, then she only hoped he would be happy because of what she had undergone, and she waited, very mild, very mute, for them to take her back to him.

No woman there possessed keys either to the doors or to the chains, or to the collars or to the wristbands, but each man carried a bunch of skeleton keys: there were three of them, one for all the doors, another for all the padlocks, the last for all the collars and bracelets. The valets had skeleton keys too. But, it being morning, the valets who had been on night-duty were asleep now, and it was one of the masters or some other valet who would come to unlock the locks. The man who entered O's cell was dressed in a suede jacket, riding breeches and boots. She did not recognize him. First, he undid the wall-chain, and O was able to lie down upon her bed. Before freeing her wrists,

24

he passed his hand between her thighs, as the masked, gloved man she had seen first in the small red room had done. Perhaps this was he. He had a bony, keen-featured face, the steady gaze one sees in the portraits of old Huguenots, and his hair was iron-grey. O met his stare for what seemed to her an interminable period, then suddenly froze: she remembered that one was forbidden to look at the masters anywhere above the belt. She shut her eyes, but too late, and heard him laugh and, as he set about freeing her hands at last, say: 'Punishment for that will come after dinner.' He spoke to Andrée and Jeanne, who had entered with him and who were waiting at attention, one on either side of the bed. Therewith he left. Andrée picked up the pillow from where it had tumbled to the floor and straightened out the coverlet which Pierre had pushed to the foot of the bed when he'd come to whip O; meanwhile Jeanne wheeled in a small table on castors, it had been placed in the hallway, now she set it beside the bed. On it were coffee, milk, sugar, bread, butter, croissants. 'Eat quickly,' said Andrée, 'it's nine o'clock, afterwards you can sleep till noon and when you hear the bell ring it will be time to get up and get yourself ready for lunch. You'll do your own bathing and arrange your hair yourself, I'll be here to make you up and lace your bodice.'

'You won't be on duty until the afternoon,' said Jeanne, 'in the library: to serve coffee, serve liqueurs, and care for the fire.'

'But you?' O asked.

'Us? We've only to look after you for the first twenty-four hours of your stay, afterwards you'll be alone and only men will deal with you. We shan't be able to talk to you, nor you to us.'

'Please stay a moment, please, and tell me —' But O's words were cut off by the opening of the door: it was her lover, and he was not alone.

It was René, dressed the way he was when he got up from bed and lit his first cigarette of the day; he was in striped pyjamas and a blue wool bathrobe: the one with the quilted silk lining they'd chosen together the year before. And his slippers were shabby, truly moth-eaten, he needed a new pair. The two women disappeared without a sound save for the rustling of silk when they lifted their skirts (all the skirts trailed some-what); the clogs couldn't be heard upon the carpeting. O, who was sitting rather precariously half on and half off the bed, one leg hanging over the edge, the other tucked up towards her body, didn't budge, although the cup suddenly began to shake in her hand and she lost hold of her croissant. 'Pick it up,' René said. That was the first thing he'd said. She posed the cup on the table, retrieved the partly-chewed croissant, and laid it by the cup. A large croissant-crumb remained on the floor, touching O's naked foot. In his turn, René stooped down and picked it up. Then he sat down next to O, bent her back-ward and kissed her. She asked him if he loved her. 'Ah, yes! I do love you,' he answered, then got up, stood her up too, and gently pressed his cool palms, then his lips, to her welts, to all her welts. Since the other man had come in with her lover, O wasn't sure whether or not she was allowed to look at him; he had turned his back for an instant and was smoking near the door. What came next could not have been an encouragement to her. 'Let's have a look at you, come here,' her lover said and, having steered her to the foot of the bed, remarked to his com-panion that he had been altogether correct, expressed his thanks, adding that it seemed only fair that he, the stranger, be the first to try her out if he were so inclined. The stranger, whom she still dared not look at, after he had glided his hands over her breasts and down her buttocks, then asked her to spread her legs. 'Do as you're told,' said René, against whose chest her back was leaning and who was holding her erect; and his right hand was caressing one of her breasts, his left held her shoulder. The stranger had seated himself on the edge of the bed, by means of the hairs growing on them had taken hold of and gradually opened the labia guarding the entrance to her crack. René nudged her forward in an effort to facilitate the task, but no, that wasn't quite it, then he understood what the other was after and slipped his right arm around her waist, thus improving his grip. Under this caress, which she had never hitherto accepted without a struggle and without an over-powering feeling of shame, from which she would escape as quickly as she could, so quickly that it scarcely had the opportunity to register its effects, and which seemed a sacrilege to her, because it seemed to her sacrilegious that her lover be on his knees when she ought to be on hers – of a sudden she sensed that she was not going to escape this caress, not this time, and she saw herself doomed. For she moaned when that strange mouth pushed aside the fold of flesh whence the inner corolla emerges, moaned when those strange lips abruptly set her afire then retreated to let a strange tongue's hot tip burn her still more; she moaned louder when strange lips seized her anew; she sensed the hidden point harden and protrude to be taken between strange teeth and tongue in a long sucking bite that held her and held her still; she reeled, lost her footing, and found herself upon her back, René's mouth upon her mouth; his two hands pinned her shoulders to the mattress whilst two other hands gripping her calves were opening and flexing her legs. Her own hands – they were behind and under her back (for at the same moment he had thrust her towards the stranger René had bound her wrists by joining the two wristbands' catches) – her hands were brushed by the sex of the man who was rubbing himself in the crease between her buttocks; that sex now rose and shot swiftly to the depths of the hole in her belly. In answer to that first blow she emitted a cry as when under the lash, acknowledged each succeeding blow with a cry, and her lover bit her mouth. It was as though snatched forcefully away that the man quit her, hurled backwards as though thunderstruck, and from his throat there also came a cry. René detached O's hands, eased her along the bed, and tucked her away under the blanket. The stranger got up and the two men went towards the door. In a flash, O saw herself immolated, annihilated, cursed. She had groaned under the stranger's mouth as never she had under René's, cried before the on-slaught of the stranger's member as never her lover had made her cry. She was profaned and guilty. If he were to abandon her, it would be rightfully. But no: the door swung to again, he was still there, was staying with her, he walked towards her, lay full length down beside her, beneath the fur blanket, slipped himself into her wet and burning belly and, holding her thus embraced, said to her: 'I love you. After I've also given you to the valets, I'll come some night and lash you till the blood flows.'

The sunshine had dissipated the mists, its rays flooded the room. But it wasn't until the midday bell rang that they woke.

O did not know what to do. Her lover was there, just as near, just as defencelessly, as sweetly abandoned as in the bed of the low-ceilinged room where almost every night ever since they'd been living together he'd come to sleep beside her. It was a big four-poster of mahogany, but without the canopy, and the posts at the head were taller than the two at the feet. He would always sleep to her left and, when he'd awake, would always reach a hand towards her legs. That was why she never wore anything but nightgowns, or, if pyjamas, never the pyjama-bottoms. And he too; she took that hand and kissed it, not daring to ask him anything. But he spoke. He told her, and as he spoke he slipped two fingers between her neck and the collar, he told her that he intended that from now on she be held in common by him and by others of his choosing and by still others whom he didn't know who were affiliated with the society that owned the château, she'd be subject to general use, as she'd been the evening before. He told her that she belonged, and was ultimately answerable to him, only to him, even if she were to receive orders from others than he, no matter whether he were there or absent, for by way of principle he concurred in no matter what she might be required to do or might be inflicted upon her; and that it was he who possessed and enjoyed her through the agency of those into whose hands he surrendered her, and this was so from the mere fact that she was surrendered to them by him, she was the gift, he the donor. She was to show obedience to them all, and greet them with the same respectfulness she greeted him, as so many images of him. Thus would he possess her as a god possessed his creatures whereupon he lays hands guised as some monster or bird, as some invisible spirit or as ecstasy itself. He did not want to, he was not going to leave her. The more he subjected her to, the more important to him she would become. The fact he gave her to others was proof thereof, proof in his eyes, it ought to be proof also in hers, that she belonged to him. He gave her so

28

as to have her immediately back, and recovered her enriched a hundredfold in his eyes, as is an ordinary object that has served some divine purpose and thereby become infused with sanctity. For a long time he had desired to prostitute her, and it was gladly he now discovered that the pleasure he reaped from it was greater than he had even dared hope, and increased his attachment to her as it did hers to him, and that attachment would be the greater, the more her prostitution would humiliate and soil and ruin her. Since she loved him, she had no choice but to love the treatment she got from him. O listened and trembled from happiness; since he loved her, she trembled, consentingly. In all likelihood he discerned her consent, for he continued: 'It's because it's so easy for you to consent that I want from you something you can't possibly consent to, even if you say yes in advance, even if you say yes now and suppose that you are actually capable of submitting to it. You won't be able to prevent yourself from saying no when the time comes. When the time comes, it won't matter what you say, you'll be made to submit, not only for the sake of the incomparable pleasure I or others will find in your submission, but so that you will be aware of what has been done to you.' O was about to reply that she was his slave and dwelt joyfully in bondage; but he halted her: 'Yesterday you were told that, so long as you are in this château, you're neither to look a man in the face nor speak to him. Nor must you look at me or speak to me any more. You're simply to be still and to obey. I love you. Get up. From now on, while you're here, you'll not open your mouth again in the presence of a man, except to scream or to bestow caresses.' So O got up. René remained stretched out on the bed. She bathed, did her hair; upon contact with her bruised buttocks the tepid water made her shiver, she had to sponge herself but not rub to avoid reviving the fiery pain. She painted her mouth, but not her eyes, powdered herself and, still naked, but with her eyes lowered, came back into the cell. René was looking at Jeanne, who had entered and who was standing quietly by the head of the bed, she too with lowered eyes, she, too, mute. He told her to dress O. Jeanne took the green satin bodice, the white petticoat, the gown, the green clogs and,

29

having hooked O's bodice in front, began to lace it up tight in back.

The bodice was stoutly whaleboned, long and rigid, something from the days when wasp-waists were in fashion, and was fitted with gussets upon which the breasts lay. The tighter it was drawn, the more prominently O's breasts rose, pushed up by the supporting gussets, and the more sharply upward her nipples were tilted. At the same time, as her waist was constricted, her womb and buttocks were made to swell out. The odd thing is that this veritable cuirass was exceedingly comfortable and, up to a certain point, relaxing. In it, one felt very upright, but, without one being able to tell just how or why unless it was by contrast, it increased one's consciousness of the freedom or rather the availability of the parts it left unencompassed. The wide skirt and the neckline, sweeping down from her shoulders to below and the whole width of her breasts, looked on the girl clad in it, not so much like an article of clothing, a protective device, but like a provocative one, a mechanism for display. When Jeanne had tied a bow in the laces and knotted it for good measure, O took her gown from the bed. It was in one piece, the petticoat tacked inside the skirt like an interchangeable lining, and the bodice, cross-laced in front and secured in back by a second series of laces, was thus, depending on how tightly it was done up, able to reproduce more or less exactly the subtler lines of the bust. Jeanne had laced it very tight, and O caught a glimpse of herself through the open door to the bathroom, her slender torso rising like a flower from the mass of green satin billowing out from her hips as if she were wearing a hoop-skirt. The two women were standing side by side. Jeanne reached to correct a pleat in the sleeve of the green gown, and her breasts stirred beneath her gauze kerchief, breasts whose nipples were long, whose halos were brown. Her gown was of yellow faille. René, who had approached the two women, said to O: 'Look.' And to Jeanne: 'Lift your dress.' With both hands she lifted the stiff crackling silk and the linen lining it to reveal a golden belly, honeysmooth thighs and knees, and a black, closed triangle. René put forth his hand and probed it slowly, with his other hand exciting the nipple of one breast, till it grew hard and yet darker. 'That's so you can see,' he told O. O saw. She saw his ironic but concentrated face, his intent eyes scanning Jeanne's half-opened mouth and the back-bent throat girdled by the leather collar. What pleasure could she, O, give him, that this woman or some other could not give him too? 'Hadn't you thought of that?' he asked. No, she'd not thought of that. She had slumped against the wall between the two doors; her spine was straight, her arms trailed limply. There was no further need for ordering her to silence. How could she have spoken? He may perhaps have been moved by her despair, for he relinquished Jeanne to take O in his arms, hugging her to him, calling her his love and his life, saying again and again that he loved her. The hand with which he was caressing her throat and neck was moist with the wetness and smell of Jeanne. And then? And then the despair in whose tide she had been drowning ebbed away: he loved her, ah yes, he did love her. He did indeed have the right to take pleasure with Jeanne, to seek it with others, he loved her. 'I love you,' she whispered in his ear, 'I love you,' in so soft a whisper he could just barely hear.

'I love you.'

It wasn't until he saw the sweetness flow back into her and the brightness into her eyes that he took leave of her, happy.

Jeanne took O by the hand and drew her into the hallway. Once again their clogs clattered on the tiles, and once again, between two doors, they discovered a valet sitting on a bench. He was dressed like Pierre, but it was by no means he. This one was tall, lean, black-haired. He rose and preceded them, directed them into an antechamber where, before a wrought-iron gate on the further side of which hung long green draperies, two other valets were waiting, white russet-spotted hounds lying at their feet. 'That's the enclosure,' Jeanne murmured.

But the valet who had been walking ahead must have overheard her, for he turned on his heel. Bewildered, O saw Jeanne grow deathly pale, let go of her hand, let go of her dress which she had been holding with her other hand, then sink to her knees upon the black flagstone floor — for the antechamber's floor was flagged in black marble. The two valets by the gate began to laugh. One of them advanced towards O, requesting her to follow him; he opened a door opposite the one they'd just come through, bowed, and bade her pass. She heard laughter, the sound of footsteps, then the door closed behind her. Never, never did she find out what had happened, whether Jeanne had been punished for having spoken and, if punished, how, or whether she had merely yielded to some caprice on the part of the valet, or if in casting herself at his knees she had been obeying some regulation, or invoking his mercy, or if she had succeeded. During her first stay at the château, lasting a fortnight, she simply noticed that, absolute as the rule of silence might be, it was rare that in the course of frequent comings and goings or at meals one was not led into breaking it, especially during the day when only in the presence of the valets, as if clothing somehow emboldened one, affording a certain self-assurance which nakedness and night-time chains and the presence of the masters would obliterate. She also noticed that whilst the slightest gesture in any way resembling an advance towards one of the masters appeared of itself, and quite naturally, perfectly inconceivable, one felt otherwise when dealing with the valets. The latter never issued orders, even though the politeness in which they couched their requests was just as implacable as any order. They were under instruction, apparently, to punish irregularities to which they alone were witness, and to punish them on the spot. Thus upon three separate occasions, first in the hallway leading to the red wing, and the other two times in the refectory they had just had her enter, O saw girls, surprised in the midst of talking, flung to the floor and lashed. It would thus seem that, despite what she had been told the first evening, one could be whipped during daylight hours, as if what went on with the valets wasn't to be counted, as if these were matters that were left to their discretion. Broad day gave their costume a curious and threatening aspect. Some of them wore black stockings, and, instead of the red jacket over the white frill-shirt, a soft red silk shirt, puckered at the neck, wide in the sleeve, tight at the wrist. It was one of these who, the eighth day, at noon, whip already in his fist, came over to near where O was sitting and bade rise from her stool a superb blonde Madeleine with breasts of milk and roses: a moment before, that lovely girl had smiled at O and said something to her, but so rapidly that O had not understood. Even before he touched her shoulder she was already on her knees, her so very white hands fluttering under the black silk, drawing out the still drowsing sex, drawing it to her beautiful, her gaping red mouth. That time she was not whipped. And as he was the lone supervisor in the refectory at the time, and as he closed his eyes as he accepted the proffered caress, the other girls turned to converse with their neighbours. There was, then, a way of dealing with the valets. But what was the use of this bribery? If there was any one regulation to which O had great trouble conforming, and to which she never did in the end entirely conform, it was the one forbidding women to look at the faces of the men; in as much as the same regulation applied with regards to the valets, O felt herself in constant danger, what with her devouring curiosity in connection with faces, and she was in fact whipped by this or that valet, not, it is true, every time they noticed her looking at their faces (for they took liberties in the interpretation of their instructions, and may also have placed a high enough value upon the fascination they exerted not to wish to deprive themselves, by means of a too absolute and too effective severity, of glances which never left their eyes and their mouths unless it were to descend to their sexes, their whips, their hands, then begin again), but, doubtless, every time they were moved by a desire to humiliate her. However cruelly they treated her, when they decided to treat her cruelly, she nevertheless always lacked the courage, or the cowardice, to fling herself of her own accord at their knees; they did sometimes put her to use, she underwent that, but she never solicited it. As for the rule of silence, it meant so little to her, save in regard to her lover, that she never once disobeyed it, answering by means of gestures when some other girl, taking advantage of the occasional inattention of their guards, addressed her. It was generally at meals, which were served in the room she had been shown into when the tall valet escorting them had whirled upon Jeanne. The walls were black, so were the flagstones under foot, the long table of thick glass was black as well, and each girl had a round stool upholstered in black leather to sit on. One had to hoist one's skirt in order to take one's place, and, the smooth, cool leather contacting her thighs, O was put in mind of that first moment when her lover had made her take off her stockings and panties and sit squarely down on the seat in the automobile. Inversely, when afterwards, having left the château and being dressed like anyone else but with her loins naked under her quite run-of-the-mill suit or dress, she was every time to lift her slip and skirt whenever she sat down beside her lover, it was a powerful remembrance of the château that overtook her: her breasts exposed and proffered by silken bodices, those alien hands and mouths to which nothing was to be denied, which could do as they wished with everything, and that terrible silence. Nothing however had been of such aid to her as the silence, unless it were the chains. The chains and the silence which ought to have sealed her isolated self within twenty impenetrable walls, to have asphyxiated her, strangled her, hadn't; to the contrary, they'd been her deliverance, liberating her from herself. What might have become of her had speech been accorded her and freedom granted her hands, had the faculty of free will been hers when her lover prostituted her while he looked on? She had spoken, it is true, under torture; but may one designate as words these which are only plaints and screams? Again, they often stilled her with gags. Beneath those stares, beneath those hands, beneath those sexes which raped her, beneath those lashes which tore her, she sank, lost in a delirious absence from herself which gave her unto love and loving, and may perhaps have brought her close to death and dying. She was – who? anyone at all, no one, someone else, one of the other girls, any one of them at all, being pried open and forced like her and whom she saw being pried open and forced – for, yes, she did see it, but even so she wasn't to help do the opening or the forcing.

The day which was her second day, when not twenty-four hours had elapsed since her coming there, lunch over with, she was conducted to the library and there her task was to serve coffee and tend the fire. Jeanne accompanied her – the black-haired valet had brought Jeanne back – and she was also accompanied by another girl, whose name was Monique. It was the same valet who escorted them hither; and he remained in the room, standing by the pillory to which O had been attached. The library was still deserted. Full-length French doors gave out to the west, and the autumn sun, pursuing a slow arc through a vast peaceful sky, virtually cloudless, shone upon a commode where stood an enormous spray of chrysanthemums, sulphur in hue, and smelling of earth and leaf-mold. 'Did Pierre mark you last night?' the valet enquired of O. She nodded. 'Then you ought not to hide it,' he said; 'kindly raise your dress.' He waited while she rolled up her dress behind, as Jeanne had done the evening before, and waited while Jeanne now helped her fix her dress in position. Then he told her to light the fire. O's flanks to the height of her waist, her thighs, her slender legs were framed in the cascading folds of the green silk and the white linen. The five welts had turned black. The kindling was ready beneath the logs, O had but to set a match to the straw. The sticks of apple caught at once, then the split butts of oak, which burned with tall, sparkling flames, almost colourless, almost invisible in the strong afternoon light, but their odour was rich. Another valet entered, upon the console whence the lamp had been cleared away placed a tray bearing the cups and the coffee, then withdrew. O moved to beside the console, Monique and Jeanne remained one on either side of the fireplace. It was at that moment two men entered, and now the first valet left. By his voice, O believed she was able to identify one of those who had forced her the evening before, he who had asked that access to her behind be rendered easier. Covertly, O stole a glance at him while pouring coffee into the little black and gold cups which Monique distributed with the sugar. Yes, it would have been he, this frail lad, still so young, fair-haired, with an English air about him. He was still speaking; she had no further doubt. The other was also blond, but short, broad-shouldered, and broad-faced. Both seated in the big leather armchairs, their feet by the fender, they were smoking quietly while reading their newspapers, paying no more attention to the women than they would have had no women been there. One now and again heard a soft clatter of newspaper, coals falling on the hearth. Now and again, O placed a new log on the fire. She was sitting on a cushion, the cushion was on the floor near the wood-basket; Monique and Jeanne, opposite her, were also sitting on the floor. Their spread skirts overlapped. Monique's was dark red. All of a sudden, but not before an hour had passed, the blond youth summoned Jeanne, then Monique. He told them to bring the hassock (it was the hassock upon which O had been stretched belly down the evening before). Monique did not await further instructions; she knelt, bent, squeezing her breasts against the surface of fur, and gripped the corners of the hassock hard with both hands. When the youth had Jeanne lift the red skirt, Monique lay completely still. Jeanne had then, and he gave her the order in the most brutal terms, to undo his garment and in both hands take that sword of flesh which had so cruelly pierced O, once at least. His member swelled and stiffened between the shut palms, and O saw those same hands, Jeanne's little hands, lay Monique's thighs aspread and, with little jerks which made him pant, the boy gradually insert himself. The other man, who had been looking on in silence, crooked his finger at O, who approached him, and without diverting his attention having tipped her forward over one of the arms of his chair – and her raised skirt offered him a full view of the whole length of her behind – he took hold of her womb with his whole hand. It was thus René found her when, a minute later, he opened the door. 'Don't allow me to disturb you, please,' he said and he took his place on the cushion O had been occupying by the hearth before she had been summoned. He watched her closely and smiled each time the hand holding her, probing her, emerged and, working ever deeper, simultaneously explored her womb and her anus, which opened ever wider until at last she moaned, unable to restrain herself longer. Monique had long since recovered her feet, Jeanne was tending the fire in O's stead; René kissed her hand when she brought him a glass of whisky, which he sipped without removing his eyes from O. The man who was still toying with her then spoke: 'She's yours?'

'Yes,' replied René.

'James is right, you know,' said the other, 'she is too tight. That's got to be fixed.'

'As you like,' said René, rising. 'You're a better judge of this than I.' And he rang.

Thereafter, for eight days in succession, between nightfall when her services in the library came to an end and the hour in the evening, eight o'clock or ten, ordinarily, when she was taken back there – when she was taken back there, chained and naked under her red cape – O wore, inserted in her anus and held in place by three little chains attached to a leather belt encircling her haunches, held, that is to say, in such a manner that the play of her internal muscles was unable to dislodge it, an ebonite rod fashioned in the shape of an uprisen male sex. One little chain followed the crease between her buttocks, the two others went round to the front, following the fold between buttock and thigh, and rose on either side of her belly's triangle so that, were there anyone who wished to, she could be conveniently penetrated there. When René had rung it was to have a servant bring the coffer in one of whose compartments was an assortment of little chains and belts, and in another a selection of these rods, the choice ranging from the thinnest to the thickest sizes. They were all alike insofar as they flared at the base, this being to make certain that they'd not ride up and become lost in the body for, if this were to happen, the muscular ring would have contracted, whereas the object was, precisely, to keep that ring open and to stretch it. Thus was she spread, and spread wider every day for, every day, James, who had her kneel down or rather lie prostrate and who looked on while Jeanne or Monique or whoever else it was who happened to be there introduced and secured the rod he had picked out, picked out a thicker one. At dinner, which the girls took together in the same refectory, but after they had bathed, and nude and made up, O would still be wearing it; and, thanks to the chains and the belt, everyone could see that she was wearing it. It was not removed except by Pierre, and then not until the moment when he came to chain her, whether to the wall for the night if no one were calling for her, or her hands behind her back if he was to conduct her back to the library. Rare were the nights when someone did not present himself to make use of this passage which was so fast becoming so easy of thoroughfare, although remaining narrower than the other, needless to say. At the end of a week there was no further need of an instrument, and her lover told O he was happy now that she was doubly open, and, said he, he would see to it that she remained that way. At the same time, he notified her that he was leaving and that during the next seven days she was to spend at the château before he returned to fetch her back with him to Paris she'd not see him. "But I love you," he added, "I love you. Don't forget me."

Forget him! Ah, how could she ever? He was the hand that blindfolded her eyes, the whip the valet Pierre wielded, he was the chain above her bed and the stranger who chewed her womb, and all the voices which uttered commands were his voice. Was she becoming weary? No. By dint of being outraged, it seemed as if she must become habituated to outrages, by dint of being caressed, to caresses, if not to the whip by dint of being whipped. A hideous satiety of pain and joy ought, one would have thought, to have edged her further and further along that gradually declining slope at whose lower depths are sleep and somnambulism. But to the contrary. The corset which held her upright, the chains which maintained her in subjection, silence, her sanctuary — perhaps these had something to do with it, as may have had the constant spectacle of girls being pressed to use, and even when they were not undergoing use, the spectacle of their at all times accessible bodies. The spectacle also and the awareness of her own body. Daily and, as it were, ritualistically soiled by saliva and sperm, by sweat mingled with her own sweat, she sensed herself to be, literally, the vessel of impurity, the gutter whereof Scripture makes mention. And yet in all, those parts of her body which were the most continually offended, having become more sensitive, seemed to her to have become, at the same time, more lovely, and as though ennobled: her mouth clamped upon anonymous members, the points of her breasts hands forever

38

were fondling, and between her wideflung thighs, the twin ways leading into her belly, avenues trod by a whole wide world to pleasure. However astonishing it were, that from being prostituted her dignity might increase, the crucial point was nonetheless one of dignity. It illumined her as if from within, and one could see her calmness in her bearing, upon her countenance the serenity and imperceptible inner smile one rather guesses at than perceives in the eyes of the recluse.

When René informed her that he was leaving, night had already fallen. O was naked in her cell, waiting to be led to the refectory. For his part, her lover was dressed as usual, in the suit he wore everyday in town. When he'd taken her in his arms the rough tweed of his coat had chafed her nipples. He kissed her, lay her upon the bed, lay down beside her, his face to her face, and tenderly and slowly and gently he took her, moving to and fro now in this, now in the other of the two passages offered to him, finally spilling himself into her mouth which, when he was done, he kissed again.

'Before I go I'd like to have you whipped,' he said, 'and this time I ask your permission. Are you willing?' She was willing. 'I love you,' he repeated; 'now ring for Pierre.' She rang. Pierre chained her hands above her head by the bed-chain. When thus bound, her lover stepped up on the bed and, his face to her face, penetrated her again, told her again that he loved her, then stepped back onto the floor and signalled to Pierre. He watched her writhe and struggle, so vainly, he listened to her groans develop into screams, these into howls. When the tears had finished flowing, he dismissed Pierre. From somewhere she found the strength to tell him again that she loved him. And then he kissed her soaking face, her gasping mouth, released her bonds, put her to bed, and left.

To say that from the instant her lover had left her O began to await his return would be no overstatement: she turned into pure waiting, darkness in waiting expectation of light. In day-time she was like a painted statue whose skin is warm and smooth, whose mouth is docile, and – it was only during this interval that she held strictly to the rule – whose eyes are for-ever lowered. She made and cared for the fire, poured and passed round the coffee, lighted the cigarettes, arranged the flowers and folded up the newspapers like a little girl busy in her parents' living-room, so limpid with her exposed breast and her leather collar, her tight bodice and her prisoner's handcuffs, so demure, so yielding that it was enough for the men she served to order her to stand by them while they were violating another girl for them to want to violate her too; and that surely was why she was treated worse than ever before. Had she sinned? or had her lover, in leaving her, deliberately intended to make those to whom he lent her feel freer to dispose of her? At any rate, on the second day after his departure, the day drawing to an end and after she had just taken off her clothes and was gazing at herself in her bathroom mirror, the marks Pierre's crop had inscribed on the front of her thighs being by now almost gone, Pierre entered. Two hours still remained before dinner. He informed her that she would not dine in the common room, and bade her ready herself, nodding to the Turkish toilet in the corner where indeed he did make her squat, as Jeanne had warned her she would have to do in Pierre's presence. All the time she was there he stood contemplating her; she saw his image reproduced in the mirrors, and saw herself incapable of holding back the water which was squirting from her body. And still he waited, until she had completed her bath and finished applying her make-up. She was about to reach for her clogs and red cape when he stopped her hand, and added, binding her hands behind her back, that she needn't go to the bother, would she wait there just a moment. She perched herself on a corner of the bed. Outside, gusts of cold wind were blowing, cold rain spattered down, the poplar near the window swayed under the gale's attack. From time to time a pale wet leaf pasted itself against a windowpane. The overcast sky was dark, it was as dark as the heart of the night even though seven had not yet struck, but autumn was wearing on and the days were growing shorter. Pierre returned; in his hand he carried the same blindfold they'd used that first night to prevent her from seeing. He also had, clinking in his hand, a long chain similar to the one affixed to the wall. It appeared to O that he was hesitating as to which to put on her first, the chain or the blindfold. She watched the rain, not caring about his intentions or his uncertainties, thinking only of what René had said, that he'd return, and that she had still five days and five nights to pass, and that she didn't know where he was or if he was alone, and if he wasn't, with whom he could be. But he'd return.

Pierre had placed the chain on the bed and, without disturbing O's thoughts, fastened the black velvet blindfold over her eyes. It fitted snugly up under the ridge of her brow and exactly followed the curve of her cheeks: no possibility of a downward glance nor even of raising her eyelids. Blessed darkness like unto her own inner night-time, never had O welcomed it with such joy, oh blessed chains which bore her away from herself. Pierre attached this new chain to the ring in her collar and invited her to accompany him. She stood up, sensed that she was being tugged along, and followed. Her bare feet froze on the icy tiles, she realized that she was walking down the red wing hallway, then the ground, as cold as before, became rough; she was walking upon flagstones, sandstone, perhaps granite. Twice the valet brought her to a halt, twice she heard a key scrape in a lock and a lock click as a door closed. 'Be careful of the steps,' said Pierre, and she descended a stairway, once almost tripped. Pierre caught her in time, though, caught her round the waist. Prior to this, he had never touched her save to chain or beat her, but now here he was laying her upon the cold steps where with her pinioned hands she hung on as best she could to avoid slithering down, here he was clutching her breasts. His mouth was roving from one to the other and at the same time he was pressing himself upon her, she felt his member gradually stiffen. It was only when he was entirely satisfied that he helped her to her feet. Perspiring and trembling from cold, she finally descended the last steps, then heard him open yet another door, through which she was led, immediately feeling a thick carpet under her feet. The chain was still exerting a pull. Yet another pull on the chain and then Pierre's hands released her hands, untied the blindfold: she was in a circular and vaulted room, quite small and very low-ceilinged; the walls and vault were of unfaced stone, the joints in the masonry were visible. The chain leading to her collar was secured to an eye-bolt set in the wall about a yard above the floor and opposite the door, leaving her free to move no more than two paces in any direction. Here, there was neither a bed nor anything that might substitute for one, there was no blanket, not a scrap of covering, and only three or four cushions like the Moroccan cushions, but out of her reach and not meant for her. On the other hand, set in the niche whence shone the sole light illuminating the room, lay a wooden tray; on it were water, fruit, and bread, and these were within her reach. The heat coming from radiators which had been installed at the base of and recessed in the thickness of the walls, and which formed a sort of burning plinth all the way around her, was nevertheless not enough to overcome the damp smell of mustiness and stone which is the odour of ancient prisons and, in old castles, of uninhabited keeps. In this sultry, soundless twilight, O soon lost all track of time, for here there was neither night nor day, and never was the light turned off. Pierre or some other valet, it didn't matter which, replenished her supply of water, placed fruit and bread on the tray when none were left, and would take her to bathe in a nearby dungeon. She never saw the men who entered, because, whenever they came, they were preceded by a valet who blindfolded her and didn't remove the blindfold until they had gone. She also lost track of these visitors, of their number, and neither her gentle blindly caressing hands nor her lips were ever able to identify whom they touched. Sometimes there were several of them, most often they came singly, but every time, before she was approached, she was placed on her knees, her face to the wall, her collar fastened to the same bolt to which her chain was affixed, and whipped. She would lay her palms flat against the wall and press her face against the back of her hands so as to avoid being scraped by the stone; but it lacerated her knees and breasts. She also lost track of the whippings and of her screams; the vault muffled them. She waited. All of a sudden, time stopped standing still. In the very midst of her velvety, anaesthetic night-time she felt her chain being detached. She'd been waiting about three months, about three days, or ten days, or

42

ten years. She felt herself being swathed in some heavy cloth, and someone taking her under the shoulders and under the legs; felt herself being lifted and borne away. She found herself in her cell again, lying underneath her black fur covering; it was early in the afternoon, her eyes were open, her hands were free, and there was René sitting beside her, caressing her hair. 'Come, dress yourself,' he said, 'we're going.'

She took one last bath, he brushed her hair, handed her powder and her lipstick. When she came back into her cell, her suit, her blouse, her slip, her stockings, her shoes lay on the foot of the bed, her handbag and her gloves too. There was even the coat she put on over her suit when the weather began to get cold, and a square of silk she wore to protect her neck, but no garter-belt, no panties. She dressed herself slowly, rolling her stockings to just above the knee, and didn't put on her jacket, for it was very warm in the cell. That was the moment when there entered a man who, the first evening, had explained what would be expected of her. He undid the collar and the wristbands which had held her captive for a fortnight. Was she freed of them? or did she feel something missing? She said not a word, hardly daring touch her fingers to her wrists, not daring raise them to her neck. He then asked her to choose, from amongst all those identical rings he was presenting to her in a little wooden case, the one which would go on the ring-finger of her left hand. They were curious, these rings, made of iron, the inner surface was of gold; the signet was massive, shaped like a knight's shield, convex, and in gold niello bore a device consisting of a kind of three-spoked wheel, each spoke spiraling in towards the hub, similar, all in all, to the sun-wheel of the Celts. She tried one, then another, and, by forcing it a little, found that it fitted her perfectly. It felt heavy on her hand, and the gold gleamed almost secretively in the polished iron's dull grey. Why iron? and why gold? And this device she didn't understand? But it wasn't possible to talk in this room, with its red hangings, with its chain still hanging over the bed, in this room where the black blanket, rumpled once again, dragged on the floor, where the valet Pierre could enter, was going to enter, was bound to, absurd in his operetta costume and in the fleecy light of November. She was mistaken, Pierre didn't enter.

René had her put on her suit jacket and her long gloves that reached up over the ends of the sleeves. He took her scarf, her bag, and folded her coat over his arm. The heels of her shoes made less noise on the hallway floor than her clogs had, the doors were shut, the antechamber empty. O held her lover's hand. The stranger who accompanied them opened the grilled gate Jeanne had said was the enclosure gate and which neither valets nor dogs were guarding now. He raised one of the green velvet curtains and had them both go through. The curtain fell back again. The grilled gate was heard to swing to. They were alone in another antechamber; beyond them stretched the garden. They had now only to go down a short flight of steps, and there in the drive was the car, O recognized it. She sat down next to her lover who was at the wheel, and they started. When they'd gone through the main gateway, which was wide open, and gone on a hundred yards or so further, he stopped to kiss her. It was just before a peaceful little village they came to a moment or two later that O saw the signpost. On it was painted: Roissy.

II

SIR STEPHEN

The Ile Saint-Louis apartment O lived in was in the attic storey of an old building on a southern quay by the Seine. The rooms were mansarded, spacious and low, and the two of them that were on the façade side each opened out upon a balcony inset between sloping sections of roof. One of these last was O's bedroom; the other – where, on one wall, full-length bookcases framed the fireplace – served as a living-room, as a study and could, if need be, function temporarily as a bedroom: there was a broad divan before the two windows, and a large antique table in front of the fireplace. Were her dinner-guests too numerous, they would eat here instead of in the small dining-room, hung in dark green serge, which faced in upon the court. Another room, also on the court, was René's, where he kept his clothes and would dress in the morning. They shared the yellow bathroom and the tiny yellow kitchen. O had a cleaning woman in every day. The rooms overlooking the court were tiled in red – the tiles were the old six-sided sort one still finds on stair-treads and landings from the third floor up in old Paris hotels. Seeing them again caused O's heart to beat faster: they were the same as the tiles in the Roissy hallways. Her bedroom was small, the pink and black chintz curtains were drawn, the fire glistened behind the screen, the bed was made, the covers turned down.

'You didn't have a nylon blouse,' said René, 'so I bought you one.' True enough: there, unfolded on the side of the bed where O slept was a white nylon blouse, pleated, tailored, fine, like one of the garments that appear on Egyptian figurines, and nearly transparent. O tried it on: round her waist she put a thin belt to conceal the series of elastics inside, and the blouse was so sheer that the tips of her breasts turned it pink.

Everything, except for the curtains and the headboard panel overlaid with the same material and the two little armchairs upholstered in the same chintz, everything in this room was white: the walls were white, the fringe round the mahogany four-poster bed was white, so was the bearskin rug on the floor. Wearing her new white blouse, O sat down by the fire to listen to her lover. He told her that, to begin with, she mustn't think of herself as free. From now on, that is to say, she was not free; or rather she was free in one sense, only in one: to stop loving him and to leave him immediately. But if she did love him, if she were going to, then she wasn't free at all. She listened to him without saying a word, calling it fortune, calling herself happy that he wanted to prove to himself, no matter how, that she belonged to him, but thinking also that there was a naïveté in his failing to realize that the degree to which he possessed her lay beyond the scope of any proof. Perhaps, though, he did realize it, and wished only to stress it? Perhaps it gave him pleasure to stress it to her? She gazed at the fire while he talked; but he, unwilling, not daring to meet her gaze, he was looking elsewhere. He was on his feet. He was pacing to and fro, staring at the floor. He suddenly said that, before anything else, in order that she hear what he was saying he wanted her, right away, to unlock her knees and unfold her arms – for she was sitting with her knees locked together and her arms folded. So she drew up her skirt and, kneeling, but sitting back on her heels, in the posture the Carmelites or the Japanese women adopt, she waited. Except that, her knees being spread, between her parted thighs she felt the faint needling of the white bearskin's fur; no, that wouldn't do, he insisted, she wasn't opening her legs wide enough. The word *open* and the expression *open your legs,* when uttered by her lover, would acquire in her mind such overtones of restiveness and of force that she never heard them without a kind of inward prostration, of sacred submission, as if they had emanated from a god, not from him. And so she remained perfectly still, her hands, palms turned upward, resting on either side of her knees, and her pleated skirt lay in a quiet circle around her. What her lover wanted of her was simple: that she be constantly and immediately accessible. It wasn't enough for him to know that she was: to her accessibility every obstacle had to be eliminated, and by her carriage and manner, in the first place, and in the second place by the clothing she wore, she would, as it were, signify her accessibility to those who knew what these signs implied. That he continued, involved doing two things. The first of them she already knew: for on the evening of her arrival at the château it had been made clear to her that she was never to cross her legs and was to keep her lips open at all times. All this, she probably thought, meant very little (she did in fact think exactly that), but she was wrong: to the contrary, she would discover that conformance to this discipline would require a continual effort of attention which would continually remind her, when they two and perhaps certain others were together even though in the midst of the most everyday occupations and while amongst those who did not share the secret, of what in reality her condition was. As for her clothing, it was up to her to choose it and, if need be, to devise a costume which would render unnecessary that half-undressing he had submitted her to in the car while taking her to Roissy: tomorrow she would go through her clothes-closets and bureau drawers and sort out every last garter-belt and pair of panties, which she would hand over to him; he would likewise take all the brassieres, like the one whose shoulder-straps he'd had to cut in order to get it off her, all the slips she had whose upper part covered her breasts, all her blouses and dresses which didn't open in front, any of her skirts which were too narrow to be raised instantly, with a single quick motion. She'd have other brassieres, other blouses and other dresses made. Between now and then was she to go to her corset-maker with her breasts naked under her blouse or sweater? Yes, he replied, that was how she would go to her corset-maker, her breasts naked under her blouse or sweater. And if anyone were to notice and comment, she'd make whatever explanations she liked, or would make none; either way, that was her own affair and no concern of his. Now as to the rest of what he had to tell her, he preferred to wait a few days and when the next time she sat down to listen to him, he wanted her to be dressed in the way she should be. In the little drawer of her writing-desk she'd find all the money she'd need. When he had finished speaking, she murmured : 'I love you' – pronounced those words without stirring an eyelash. It was he who added wood to the fire, lit the pink opaline lamp by the bed. Then he told O to get into bed and to wait for him, as he was going to sleep with her. When he returned, O put out her hand to turn off the light : it was her left hand and before darkness engulfed everything the last thing she saw was her ring. Propped on one elbow, lying on one hip, she saw the dull glint of iron, then touched the switch; and at that same instant her lover's low voice summoned her by her name, she went to him, he laid his whole hand upon her womb and drew her the rest of the way.

The next morning, O was in the dining room, in her dressing-gown, having just finished breakfast and alone – René had gone early and wasn't to be back until evening to take her to dinner – when the telephone rang. The phone was in her room, on the bedside table by the lamp. O sat on the floor and picked up the receiver. It was René. The cleaning-woman, he asked, had she left? Yes, she'd gone just a moment ago, after serving breakfast, and she wasn't due back until the following day.

'Have you started to go through your things?' René asked.

'I was about to,' she replied, 'but I got up very late, didn't finish my bath till noon –'

'Are you dressed?'

No, I'm in my nightgown and bathrobe.'

'Set the receiver down – no, don't hang up, set it on the bed. Take off your nightgown and your bathrobe.'

O obeyed, a little hastily, for the receiver slipped off the bed and fell onto the white rug; still more hastily, fearing the connection had been broken, she snatched it up, said : 'Hello.'

No, it wasn't broken.

'Are you naked?' René asked.

'Yes,' she said. 'Where are you calling from?'

He didn't reply to her question. 'You've still got your ring on?'

She had it on. Then he told her to stay as she was until he returned and, staying that way, to put the things she was discarding into a suitcase; and he hung up.

It was past one o'clock, the weather was clear. A patch of sunlight fell on the rug where, after taking them off, she had let fall the white nightgown and the velvet corduroy bathrobe, pale green in colour, like the hulls of fresh almonds. She collected them and started towards the bathroom to hang them up in a closet; on the way she encountered a three-sided mirror formed by a glass mounted on a door and two others, one straight ahead and one on the right, in a bend in the hall: she encountered her reflection: she was naked save for the green leather clogs of the same green as her bathrobe and not much darker than the clogs she had worn at Roissy, and the ring. She was no longer wearing collar or leather wristbands, and she was alone, sole spectator to herself. Be that as it may, she had never felt so utterly subject to a foreign will, never so utterly a slave nor so happy to be one. When she bent to open a drawer, she saw her breasts sway softly. She was almost two hours at laying out on the bed the clothes she was supposed next to put in the suitcase. First of all, the panties; well, there was no problem here, they all went into a pile by the bedpost. The brassieres? The same thing, they all had to go: for they all crossed behind and hooked at the side. But she did see that the same model could perfectly well do if the catch were brought round to the front, just under the hollow between her breasts. Out went the garter-belts too, but she hesitated getting rid of the rose satin corset which laced up the back and which so closely resembled the bodice she'd worn at Roissy. So she set it aside, on the dressing-table. René'd decide. He'd also decide about the sweaters which, without exception, were the slipover sort and tight around the neck, hence unopenable. But they could, why not? they could be pulled up from the waist by anyone wanting to get at her breasts. Well, she'd wait and see. On the other hand, there was no doubt about the full-length slips:

4

49

they were in a heap on the bed. In the bureau drawer remained one half-slip, black crêpe hemmed with fine lace at the bottom; she used to wear it beneath a pleated circular sun's-ray skirt in loose-woven wool, light enough to be transparent. She'd have to have other half-slips, light-coloured and short. She also realized that she'd have to give up wearing slipover dresses, but that she might be able to get the same effect from a dress which buttoned all the way down in front and it might be possible to have a built-in slip made which would unbutton at the same time the dress was unbuttoned. In connection with the half-skirts there wasn't likely to be any trouble, nor with the dresses, but what in the world would her dressmaker say about these underthings? She'd tell her she wanted a removable lining because she was sensitive to the cold. Come to think of it, she *was* sensitive to the cold and she suddenly wondered how, with the light clothing she usually wore, she ever managed out-of-doors in the winter. Finally, when she'd finished the job, and from her wardrobe salvaged only those of the blouses which buttoned in front, her black pleated half-slip, her coats of course, and the suit she'd worn back from Roissy, she went to make some tea. She moved up the thermostat in the kitchen; the woman hadn't remembered to fill the living-room firewood basket and O knew that her lover would be delighted to find her in the living-room by the fire when he came home that evening. Out in the corridor there was a big wood-box; she filled the basket, carried it into the living-room, and got a fire going. Thus did she wait, curled up in a big chair, the tea-tray next to her, thus did she await his return; but this time, as he had ordered, she awaited him naked.

The first difficulty O met with was at work. Difficulty? Not quite; rather, she met with astonishment. O worked in the fashion branch of a photograph agency. Which meant that, in the studio where they posed hour after hour, she took the pictures of the strangest – and prettiest-looking – girls whom *couturiers* had selected to model their gowns. They were astonished, or at least surprised, that O had extended her vacation so far into the autumn and, in so doing, had absented herself at the very period when professional activity was at its height, when new styles were about to be released. That surprised them. But they were truly astonished at the change that had taken place in her. At first glance, you couldn't tell in just what way, but you sensed there'd been some sort of a change, and the more you looked at her, the surer of it you were. She stood straighter, her gaze was clearer, sharper, but what was downright striking was this faultless immobility when she was still and, when she moved, the measure, the sureness in her movements. Previously, she'd always dressed soberly, as working girls do when their work resembles men's work, but so cleverly that sobriety seemed quite right for her; and owing to the fact that the other girls, who constituted the very object of her work, had clothing and adornments by way of occupation and vocation, they were quick to detect what other eyes might not have seen. Sweaters worn next to the skin and which so softly outlined her breasts – René had ended up permitting sweaters – pleated skirts which, when she turned, swirled so readily, these took on the quality of a discreet uniform, so regularly was O seen wearing them. 'Very little-girl,' and that in a teasing manner, from a blond green-eyed mannequin with high Slavic cheek-bones and the Slavic olive tint, 'but you're wrong about the garterbelt, you're not going to do your legs any good wearing elastic-bands all the time' – for O, in front of her and without paying attention, had sat down a little too quickly and at an angle upon the arm of a heavy leather-upholstered chair and her skirt had, for a moment, flown up. The tall girl had caught a flash of naked thigh above the rolled-down stocking stopping just above the knee. O had seen her smile, smile so curiously that, at that very instant, she'd wondered what the girl had supposed or perhaps understood. She pulled her stockings up tight, first one stocking, then the other (it wasn't as easy keeping them tight that way as when they mounted to mid-thigh and when garters held them in place), and replied, as if to justify herself: 'It's practical.'

'Practical for what?' Jacqueline said.

'I don't like garter-belts,' O answered. But Jacqueline wasn't listening to her; her eyes fixed on the iron ring.

During the next few days O made some fifty photographs

51

of Jacqueline. They were like none she had ever taken before. Perhaps she had never had such a model before. In any case, she had never been able to extract anything quite like this impassioned meaningfulness from a face or a body. Yet she had undertaken no more than to highlight the silks, the furs, the laces, with the fairy-tale loveliness, the suddenly awakened Sleeping Beauty surprise which swept over Jacqueline no matter what she was wearing, the simplest blouse or the most elegant mink. Her hair was cut short, it was thick and blonde, faintly waved, and, as they were readying the shot, she'd bend her head ever so slightly towards her left shoulder, leaning her cheek against the upturned collar of her fur, if she was wearing a fur. O caught her once that way, smiling and sweet, her hair faintly lifted as though by some gentle breeze, and her soft but hard cheek grazing silver-fox, as grey and delicate as fresh firewood ash. Her lips were parted, her eyes half-closed. Under the cool brilliance of glossy paper one would have thought this the picture of some blessed victim of a drowning; pale, so very pale. From the negative O had made a high-key print all in soft greys. She had taken another photograph of Jacqueline, even more stunning than the first: this one was side-lit, her shoulders bare, her delicately-shaped head and delicately-featured face too enveloped in a large-mesh black veil, that surmounted by absurd-looking egret feathers wafting upward in a crown of mist or smoke; she was wearing an immense gown of heavy silk and brocade, red, like what brides wore in the Middle Ages, going to within a few inches of the floor, flaring at the hips, tight at the waist, and whose armature sketched her breasts. Nobody ever wore such dresses anymore, it was what the *couturiers* called a show-gown. The very high-heeled sandals were also of red silk. And all the while Jacqueline was there before O in this dress and in those sandals and that veil, which was like a suggestion of mask, in mind O completed the image, modified it according to a prototype she had: just a shade of this, a shade of that – the waist constricted a little more tightly, the breasts a little more sharply uplifted – and it was the Roissy dress, the same dress Jeanne had been wearing, the same heavy silk, shining, smooth, cascading, the silk one

52

seizes in great handfuls and raises when one's told to . . . And, yes, Jacqueline had hold of handfuls of it and was lifting it as she stepped down from the platform where she had been posing for a quarter of an hour. It was the same rustling, the same dry-leaves crackling. Nobody ever wears such dresses any-more? Oh, but there are still some who wear them. Round her neck, Jacqueline also was wearing a golden choker, two golden bracelets on her wrists. O caught herself in the midst of imagin-ing that she'd be lovelier with a collar and with bracelets of leather. And now, doing something she'd never done before, she followed Jacqueline out into the large dressing-room, ad-jacent to the studio, where the models dressed and made up and where they left their clothes and make-up when they left. She leaned against the doorjamb, her eyes riveted upon the hairdresser's mirror before which Jacqueline, still wearing her dress, had sat down. The mirror was so tall – it reflected the entirety of the room, and the dressing-table was an ordinary table surfaced with black glass – that O could see both Jac-queline's and her own image, and the image also of the dress-ing-assistant who was detaching the egret plumes and removing the tulle veil. Jacqueline herself undid her choker, her naked arms lifted like two swans' necks; a trace of sweat glistened under her armpits, which were shaven (why shaven? What a pity, thought O, she is so fair), and O could smell the keen, pungent odour, somewhat vegetable and wondered what per-fume Jacqueline ought to be wearing – what perfume they'd give Jacqueline to wear. Then Jacqueline undid her bracelets, posed them on the glass table-top where, for a fleet instant, they made a clicking like chains clicking. She was so fair-haired that her skin was of a darker hue than her hair, bistre, beige, like fine sand just after the tide has retreated. On the photo, the red silk would come out black. At that same mo-ment, the thick eyelashes Jacqueline painted only to satisfy the requirements of her job and reluctantly, lifted, and in the mir-ror O caught a glance so keen, so steady, that, the while unable to remove her own she sensed a warmth flow into her cheeks. That was all, just one glance.

'I beg your pardon, I must undress.'

'Excuse me,' O murmured, and closed the door.

The next day she took home the prints made the day before, not knowing whether she did or didn't desire to show them to her lover; with him she was dining out that evening. While making up before the dressing-table in her room, she gazed at them and would now and then interrupt what she was doing to touch her finger to the photo and trace the line of an eyebrow, the contour of a smile. But when she heard the sound of a key in the front-door lock, she slipped the prints away into the drawer.

For two whole weeks O had been entirely taken up with work, and wasn't getting used to it, and then, coming home one evening from the studio, she found a note from her lover asking her to be ready at eight to join him and a friend for dinner. A car would be sent to fetch her, the chauffeur would come to the door. In a postscript he asked her to wear her fur jacket, dress entirely in black (*entirely* was underlined), and take care to make up and perfume herself in exactly the way she had at Roissy. It was already six. Entirely in black, and for dinner – and it was mid-December, cold outside, that meant black silk stockings, black gloves, pleated skirt, her thick knitted sweater or the crêpe page-boy jacket. She thought it had better be the page-boy jacket. It was padded and quilted in large squares, reinforced and stiff from collar down to waist, like the narrow coats men wore in the sixteenth century, and the reason why it moulded her bust so perfectly was because the soutien-gorge was fitted inside. It was lined with the same faille, and the basques, split, reached down to her hips. It was black everywhere except for the large golden hooks, which looked like the hooks on children's snow-boots, opening and closing with a scraping noise made by the large flat clasps. After she had laid her costume out on the bed and at the foot of the bed set her black suede shoes with platform soles and needle-heels, O thought it the strangest thing in the world to find herself in her own bathroom, free and alone after her bath, and now meticulously making up and perfuming herself, as at Roissy. Her cosmetics weren't the same which were used there, however. In the drawer of her dressing-table she found some cake-rouge which she'd never used before but which managed to accentuate the halo round her nipples. It was one of those rouges one barely sees when applying it, but whose colour deepens later on. At first she thought she'd applied too much, wiped off a little with alcohol – it didn't wipe off easily or well – and began again: she achieved a dark peony-red: two flowers blossomed at the tips of her breasts. In vain she sought to rouge the lips the fleece of her belly hid, the cake-rouge refused to take on them. Amongst the various lipsticks she had in the same drawer she finally located one of those kissproof rouges which she didn't like to use because they were too dry and remained too long on the lips. But for present purposes the kissproof variety worked well. She did her hair, finished her face, then perfumed herself. In an atomizer which expelled a thick spray was a perfume whose name she didn't know, but which had a dry-wood or poignant, somewhat wild-plant odour. The mist melted upon her skin, flowed over the hair under her arms and at her belly, hanging in tiny droplets. At Roissy O had learned not to be in a hurry: she perfumed herself three times, each time letting the perfume dry on her body. First she put on her stockings, then her high-heeled shoes, then the half-slip and the skirt, then the jacket. She put on her gloves, took her bag. In her bag were her compact, her lipsticks, a comb, her key, one thousand francs. Gloves on her hands, she took her fur wrap from the armoire, checked the time by her bedside clock: it was a quarter before eight. She sat down on the edge of the bed and, her eyes fixed on the dial of the little clock, in perfect stillness awaited the sound of the doorbell. When she heard it and rose to leave, before turning out the light, she glanced at the dressing-table mirror and saw her reflected gaze: bold, mild, and docile.

Upon opening the door to the little Italian restaurant before which the car had stopped, the first person she saw was René, at the bar. He smiled tenderly, took her hand, and turning toward a sort of grey-haired athlete, introduced her, in English to Sir Stephen H. O was offered a stool beween the two men and as she was about to seat herself, René whispered

to her to be careful not to wrinkle her dress. He helped her
slide her skirt over the edge of the stool, and she felt the cold
leather against her skin, the cold metal rim against the lower
part of her womb itself, for she dared not sit all the way down
at first, dreading lest if, she did, she yield to the temptation to
cross one leg over the other. Her skirt hung down all the way
around her. Her right heel was hooked on one of the
rungs of the stool, the tip of her left foot touched the floor. The
expressionless Englishman, who without saying a word had simply made an imperceptible bow, had not taken his eyes off
her; she noticed him study first her knees, her hands next, finally her lips – but study them so tranquilly, and with an attention so precise and so sure of itself, that O felt herself being
weighed and hefted for the instrument she very well knew she
was, and it was as though under the pressure of his gaze
and so to speak in spite of herself that she removed her gloves :
she knew that he would speak as soon as her hands were bare
– because her hands were unusual, resembling those of a youth
rather than those of a woman, and because, on the third finger
of her left hand, she wore the iron ring with the triple golden
spiral. But no. He didn't say anything, he smiled : he'd seen the
ring. René was drinking his second Martini and O the grape-
fruit juice René had ordered for her; as he set down his glass
he said that unless O were otherwise disposed, she would do
him the kindness of concurring in their view that it might be
better to go downstairs to eat, for the dining-room below was
smaller and sure to be quieter than this one which, on the
ground floor, was hardly separated from the bar.

'Certainly,' said O who had already picked her bag and
gloves up from where she had laid them on the bar.

Sir Stephen, helping her down from the stool, offered her
his right hand in which she laid hers, and finally addressing
her directly, did so to observe that such hands were made for
irons, so admirably did iron become her. But as he said it in
English there was a faint ambiguity in the terms, and one
might be in doubt whether to understand if he was alluding
only to the metal or if not also, and above all, to chains.

The downstairs was a simple *cave*, whitewashed but airy

and gay, with, it turned out, only four tables, one of which was occupied by people who were finishing their meal. On the walls they had fresco-like representations of *l'Italie gastronomique* done in soft ice-cream colours: vanilla, raspberry, pistachio; looking about her, O decided to ask for an ice-cream dessert, with pralines and whipped-cream. For she felt in a happy, light-hearted mood, under the table René's knee touched hers, and when he spoke, she knew he was talking on her behalf. He too was gazing at her lips. Her request for ice-cream was granted but to coffee they said no. Sir Stephen proposed that O and René join him for coffee at his home. All three had dined lightly, almost sparingly, and O remarked to herself that, if the men had drunk exceedingly little, she'd been allowed to drink even less: half a flask of chianti had sufficed for the three of them. And they had eaten quickly too: it was only a few minutes after nine.

'I dismissed the chauffeur,' said Sir Stephen. 'René, will you drive? I think the simplest thing would be to go straight to my place.'

René took the wheel, O sat next to him, Sir Stephen next to her. The automobile was a large Buick, providing ample space for three in the front seat.

After the Alma circle, the Cours de la Reine was clearly visible through the leafless branches of the trees; and the place de la Concorde was scintillating and dry, overhung by those dark clouds promising snow which can't make up its mind to fall. O heard a click and felt warm air climb up along her legs: Sir Stephen had switched on the heater. René followed the Right Bank a little while longer, then took the Pont Royal to the Left Bank: between the bridges' stones arches the Seine looked as immobile as stone, and black. When she'd been fifteen, her best friend, who'd been thirty and with whom she'd been in love, had worn a ring with a huge hematite set in a cluster of diamonds. O had always wanted a necklace of those black stones, but without diamonds, a tight-fitting necklace, a choker, who knows? a very tight-fitting choker, perhaps that's what she'd always wanted. But the collars they gave her now – no they didn't give them – would she have exchanged them for the hematite necklace, the choker, the one she'd cherished in her adolescent's dreams? Once again she saw the mean, shoddy room Marion had taken her to, behind the Turbigo intersection, and visualized how she, O, not Marion, had undone her two large schoolgirl's braids after Marion had undressed her and had her lie down on the iron bedstead. When caressed Marion was beautiful and it's perfectly true that eyes can look like stars; hers had resembled trembling blue stars. René parked the car. O didn't recognize this little street, one of those running between the rue de l'Université and the rue de Lille.

Sir Stephen's apartment was at the far end of a court-yard in a wing of an old *hôtel*, and the rooms were laid out in a line, one opening into the next. The furthest from the entry was the largest and the most restful, furnished in dark English mahogany and pale silks, striped yellow and grey.

'I shan't ask you to tend the fire,' Sir Stephen said to O, 'but this couch is for you. Sit down, would you please, René will see to the coffee, I should like you simply to listen to me.'

The broad damascus-covered couch was set perpendicular to the fireplace, opposite windows overlooking a garden and facing away from other windows, on the other side of the room, which overlooked the courtyard. O removed her wrap and hung it over the back of the couch. When she turned, she saw that her lover and Sir Stephen, both standing, were waiting for her to comply with Sir Stephen's invitation. She laid her bag near the fur wrap, removed her gloves. When, oh when she wondered, when ever would she find the one rapid and furtive and unobtrusive gesture whereby she would be able to lift her skirts at the same moment she sat down so as to prevent anyone from noticing, no one would notice, the gesture which would allow her to forget her nakedness, to take it and her submission for granted? It would not at any rate be so long as René and this stranger stared at her in silence, as they were doing. She finally yielded. Sir Stephen placed fuel on the fire, René suddenly passed behind the couch and, seizing O's neck and hair, drew her head against the back of the couch and kissed her mouth, kissed her for so long and so profoundly that she lost her breath, gasped, and felt something melt in her belly, and burn. When he released her it was to say that he loved her; so saying, he took hold of her again, immediately. O's hands, idle, empty, the palms helplessly turned upward, lay on the black dress spread like a corolla around her; Sir Stephen had approached and when René finally let her go and she opened her eyes, it was the keen grey gaze of the Englishman they encountered. Bewildered as she still was, and dizzy from joy, she was nevertheless very able to see that he was looking at her admiringly, and that he desired her. Who could have resisted her moist, half-opened mouth, her swollen lips, her white neck flung back against the black collar of her page-boy jacket, her wide-open and bright eyes, her steady, un-fugitive eyes? But Sir Stephen's single gesture was to caress her eyebrows and then her lips, softly, with the tip of his finger. Then he took a place opposite her, on the other side of the fireplace, and when René had also seated himself in an arm-chair, he began to speak.

'I don't believe René has ever spoken to you of his family. You may perhaps know, however, that, before wedding his father, René's mother was married to an Englishman who had a son by a first marriage. I am that son, I was brought up by René's mother until the day she left my father. Thus, strictly speaking, I am in no way related to René, and yet we are brothers, after a fashion. René loves you, I know it. I would have known it even had he not told me so, even if he had not stirred: it's quite enough to see the way he looks at you. I also know that you are one of those who have been at Roissy, and I dare say you will be going back there. Theoretically, I have the right to do as I like with you, the ring you are wearing gives it to me as to anyone else who, seeing it, knows what it signifies; but the simple exercise of my right is one thing, what we want from you is quite another and more serious. I say "we" because, as you observe, René isn't saying anything: he wishes me to address you in both his behalf and mine. If we are brothers, I am the elder, he being ten years younger than I. Between the two of us there also exists a freedom of such long standing and of such an absolute character that what belongs to me has always been his, and contrariwise. Will you consent to common ownership? I do very much hope that you will, and I am posing the question because your acquiescence will require much more on your part than did passive endurance of an imposed condition. We should like to move beyond that stage, you see. Before replying, consider that I am merely and cannot be other than another form of your lover : thus, you will always have a single master. A somewhat more redoubtable master, I rather expect, than the men to whom you were surrendered at Roissy; for I'll constantly be there. And besides,' Sir Stephen concluded, couching this final phrase in English, 'I have a fondness for habits and ritual.'

His calm, even voice pierced an absolute silence. Even the flames in the fireplace danced soundlessly. O was as though riveted to the couch, like a butterfly impaled by a pin, a long pin of words and glances which penetrated the middle of her body and nailed her naked and attentive loins to the warm silk. She no longer seemed mistress of her breasts, nor of the nape of her neck, nor of her hands; but of one thing she was certain : the object of those habits and that ritual was going to be the possession of, amongst other parts of her body, the long thighs that were hidden under her black skirt and that, already, beforehand, were open. The two men were facing her. René was smoking, but had lit one of those lamps which counteract smoke, and the air in the room, purified by the wood fire, had the cool smell of night-time.

'Will you answer me now?' Sir Stephen enquired. 'Or would you like me to tell you a little more?'

'If you give your consent,' René put in, 'I myself will explain Sir Stephen's preferences to you –'

'My expectations rather,' Sir Stephen corrected him.

Consent, O was telling herself, consent wasn't the difficult part, and it was then she realized that neither of the men had for one instant anticipated the possibility of her not consenting; neither had she. Speaking, saying anything – that was the difficult part. Her lips were afire, her mouth was dry, the saliva wasn't there anymore, an anguish composed of fear and desire had her by the throat, and the hands she had recovered control of were cold and clammy. If she could have but closed her eyes, at least. But no, two gazes pursued hers, stalked hers; she could not elude the hunter, nor did she wish to. They drew her back towards what she thought she had left for a long time and perhaps forever at Roissy. For since her return, René had always taken her by means of caresses, caressingly, and the symbol declaring that she belonged to whomsoever knew its secret had simply not happened to produce any consequences: either, she had not encountered anyone who knew it, or else, if she had, those who knew the secret had not betrayed the fact – the one person she could possibly suspect was Jacqueline (and if Jacqueline had been at Roissy, why didn't she too have a ring on her finger? And, furthermore, if Jacqueline did know the secret, what rights over O did knowing it confer upon her?) Did she have to move in order to speak? But she couldn't move of her own accord – an order would probably have brought her to her feet in an instant, but this time what they wanted from her was not obedience to an order, it was that, voluntarily, she come forward and acknowledge herself a slave and surrender herself as such. That's what they called her avowal of consent. She recalled that she had never said anything to René except 'I love you' and 'I am yours.' It seemed as if they wanted to have her talk today, and in so many plain words accept what up until now only her silence had accepted. In the end she straightened her back and, as if what she had to say was smothering her, unfastened the upper clasps on her tunic, baring herself down to the cleft between her breasts. Then she stood up, all the way up. Her knees and hands were trembling. 'I am yours,' she told René at last, 'I'll be what you want me to be.'

'No,' said he, 'you're to be ours. Repeat it after me: "I belong to both of you, I will be what both of you want me to be." '

Sir Stephen's hard grey eyes remained fixed upon her, René's eyes remained fixed upon her; under those gazes she went to her doom, slowly repeating the phrases her lover dictated to her, dutifully substituting the pronouns: it was like a grammar exercise: 'You acknowledge my and Sir Stephen's right . . .' said René, and, in as clear a voice as she could muster, O responded: 'I acknowledge your and Sir Stephen's right . . .' The right to dispose of her body as they saw fit, in whatever place and in whatever manner they pleased, the right to keep her in chains, the right to flog her as a slave is flogged or as is one sentenced to punishment, for whatever the cause or for none save that of their pleasure, the right to ignore her pleadings and outcries, if they were to make her cry out. 'I believe,' said René, 'that it is at this point Sir Stephen would like me, and you yourself, to entrust you into his keeping, and that he would like me to present you an outline of what he expects of you.' O listened to her lover and the words he had addressed to her at Roissy returned to her mind: they were almost identical to these. But then, at Roissy, she had, while listening to them, been pressed up against him, had been shielded by a feeling of the fantastic, of the incredible, had been able to hide behind the feeling that she was undergoing some other existence or perhaps that she wasn't existing at all. Dream or nightmare, prison scenery, party costumes, people in masks, all this had denied reality, transported her out of the realm of her everyday life and conveyed her far away to where there is no certain gauging of time. At Roissy she had felt herself to be as one is at night-time, deep in a dream one has dreamt before and which begins anew: sure that the dream exists, sure that it will come to an end, one would like to have it end because one's afraid of being unable to bear it, and one would like it to continue because one's afraid of not finding out how it all ends. Well, here was the ending, right here, just where one would never have supposed it would be, where she wasn't expecting it, and in the most unexpected of all imaginable forms (granting of course, as she now said to herself, granting that this was indeed the ending and that there wasn't some other ending hidden behind it, or still a third ending hidden behind the second one). What distinguished this ending was the way it made recollection tip into the present; and the way, also that what had formerly had no reality save in a closed circle, in a sealed-off domain, was all of a sudden getting ready to contaminate all the habits and all the circumstances of her daily life; and this ending both upon her and within her, was no longer to be content with outward signs – naked loins, laced-up bodices, an iron ring – but to require the thoroughgoing accomplishment of an act. It was very true that René had never whipped her, and the only difference between the period before he had taken her to Roissy and the period that had begun with their return, was that he now did with her mouth and behind what in the past he had only done (and was continuing to do), with her belly. At Roissy, she had never known whether the beatings she had so regularly received had been, even just once, administrated by him (when there had been occasion for doubt about the matter, when she was blindfolded or those dealing with her masked), but she didn't believe so. In all likeli-hood, his pleasure was so immense in watching her bound and helpless body's vain strugglings and in hearing her screams that, in order not to miss anything of the spectacle, he would surely have refused to take a more active part in it. And so that what he was now saying amounted to virtual confession; she heard him say – so sweetly, so tenderly, without stirring in the large over-stuffed chair he was reclining in, almost lying in, one knee crossed over the other – how terribly happy he was to hand her over, how terribly happy he was that she was handing herself over to Sir Stephen, to his orders and wishes. Should Sir Stephen wish her to spend the night with him, or merely an hour, or desire her to accompany him out of Paris or to some play or concert or restaurant in Paris itself, he would telephone to her and send his car to fetch her – unless René himself came to fetch her. Today, now, it was for her to do the talking. Did she consent? But she couldn't talk.

This will they were all of a sudden asking her to express, it was the will that wills self-abandon, that says yes in advance to everything to which, oh yes, she very surely did want to say yes, but to which her body was saying no, at least insofar as the whip was concerned. For concerning the rest, if she were to be honest with herself she would have to admit that she was too shaken by the desire she read in Sir Stephen's eyes to de-ceive herself, and trembling as she was, and perhaps precisely because she was trembling, she knew she was waiting with greater impatience than he for the moment when he would touch his hands, or perhaps his lips, to her. Doubtless – obviously – it was for her to hasten that moment. Whatever her violent desire to do so whatever the courage she may have had, she suddenly felt herself weaken and as she was on the point of replying, she sank to the floor, her dress in a pool around her, and, leaden-voiced in the silence, Sir Stephen ventured it as his opinion that fear also became her. The remark was directed not to her but to René. O had the impression that he was checking an impulse, refraining from advancing upon her, and she regretted that self-control. However, she was not looking at him, her eyes were riveted upon René. She was horrified lest he detect in hers what he might very well consider a betrayal. And yet it wasn't one; for if she were to have weighed her desire to be had by Sir Stephen against her belonging to René, she'd not have hesitated a moment; she was, truthfully, allowing herself to succumb to this desire only because René had permitted her to have it and, in a certain way, to a certain extent, given her to understand that he was ordering her to have it. However, the doubt still clung in her mind : might he not be irritated to see her obey with such alacrity and so well? The least sign from him would have effaced that doubt in a trice. But he evinced no sign, confining himself to asking her, for the third time, to answer. She stammered : 'I agree to whatever the two of you may want,' then lowered her eyes to her hands which were waiting, flapped out beside her knees; then enquired, in a murmur : 'I'd like to know if I shall be whipped . . .' There was a long pause; during it, she twenty times over repented her question; during it, no one spoke. Then at last Sir Stephen said : 'Sometimes.'

Next, O heard a matchstick crack, after that, the tinkling of glasses : one of the two men was probably pouring himself some whisky. René was leaving O to her own devices. René was silent. 'Even if I consent to it now,' she said, 'even if I give my promise now, I won't be able to bear it.'

'You are simply being asked to undergo it, and if you scream, if you beg for mercy, to consent, now, ahead of time that it will be in vain,' Sir Stephen continued.

'Oh, have pity on me!' said O, 'not again, no more of that,' for Sir Stephen had risen to his feet. So also had René, he was leaning towards her, gripping her shoulders.

'Answer,' he said. 'You consent?'

She finally said that she consented. He gently helped her up and, sitting down, he had her kneel on the floor alongside him: she faced the back of the couch upon which, her arms outstretched, her eyes shut, she rested her head and chest. It was then that a memory came to her mind: several years before she had seen a curious print showing a woman kneeling, as she was, before an armchair. In the picture, the floor of the room was tiled, a child and a puppy were playing in a corner, the woman's skirts were raised, and a man standing nearby was brandishing a handful of switches, preparing to beat her. All the figures were wearing late sixteenth century costumes and the print had a title which had struck her as revolting: Family Discipline. One of René's hands held her wrists in a vice while with the other he was raising her skirts, raising them so high that she felt pleated material brush against her cheek. He was caressing her flanks, her loins, drawing Sir Stephen's attention to the twin creases dividing her vertically, and having him appreciate the softness of the flesh on the inner side of her thighs. He then placed that same hand upon her waist, squeezed to emphasize her buttocks, commanding her to open her knees further. Without a word, she did as she was told. The liberties René was taking with her body, his enthusiastic commentary upon it, Sir Stephen's replies, the coarseness of the language the two men were employing, hurled her into a fit of shame, so violent, so unexpected, that the desire she had had for Sir Stephen vanished, and she began to long for the lash as for a deliverance, to long for pain and screams as for a self-justification. But Sir Stephen's hands opened her womb, forced apart her buttocks, penetrated, released her, seized her again, caressed her until she gasped out her sighs, quaking with pleasure and humiliation, and spent, and undone. 'I leave you to Sir Stephen,' René then said, 'stay as you are, he'll send you back when he wishes.' How many times had she not, at Roissy, remained thus on her knees, waiting, prostrate in the path of chance and anybody at all? But, at Roissy, she had always been constrained, held by the wrist-bands locking her hands together, the lucky captive upon whom everything was inflicted, of whom nothing was asked. Here, it was of her own choice that she remained half-naked: the same will that would have brought her to her feet was enough to bring her body to subjection. Her promise bound her as inexorably as had leather bracelets and chains. Was it only her promise that bound her? And humiliated as she was, or rather because she was humiliated, was there not a sweetness in acquiring a value through her very humiliation, through nothing but her docile willingness to bow down, through her obedience to open herself? René gone, Sir Stephen accompanying him to the door, she waited all by herself, motionless, feeling more exposed in the solitude and in the waiting more prostituted than she had felt when the two men had been there in the room. The grey-and-yellow-striped silk covering of the couch was smooth beneath her cheek, through the nylon of her stockings she felt the carpet's nap under her knees, and upon the whole length of her leg the heat emanating from the fire to which Sir Stephen had added three logs, now burning noisily. An old clock above a commode ticked so quietly that only now was she able to make out the sound, in the stillness environing her. O listened attentively, aware of the towering absurdity, in this well-appointed and civilized drawing-room, of being in the posture she was in. From the further side of the draw curtains came the drowsy rumbling of Paris after midnight. In tomorrow morning's daylight, would she recognize the place where she had pressed her head upon the couch's cushion, would there be a mark there? Would she ever, in broad wide-awake daylight, be able to return to this same drawing-room, to be treated in the same way again? Sir Stephen had still not returned; and O, who had with such pure passivity awaited the sweet pleasure of the strangers at Roissy, was now strangling over the thought that in a minute, in ten, he'd once again lay hands upon her. But it didn't go in exactly the way she'd expected. She heard him open the door again, and shut it, and traverse the room. He remained standing awhile with his back to the fire, contemplating O; then, in a very low voice, bade her get up from where she was kneeling, and sit down. She obeyed, surprised and almost annoyed. Courteously, he brought her a jigger of whisky and a cigarette. She said no thank you to both. She then noticed that he was in a dressing-gown, in a severely simple robe of grey home-spun – the same tone of grey as his hair. His hands were long and thin and sinewy, his nails, trimmed short and flat, were very white. He intercepted O's gaze, she reddened; these were the selfsame hands, tough and insistent, which had laid hold of her body, and which now she dreaded, and which now she hoped for. But he didn't come near her. 'I should like to have you undress, entirely,' said he. 'But first without getting up, merely unfasten your tunic.' O unfastened the large gilt clasps and, wriggling her shoulders, slipped out of the close-fitting jacket; she put it at the far end of the couch, where her fur wrap, her bag and her gloves already were. 'Toy with your nipples, caress them just a bit,' said Sir Stephen, who added that she would have to use a darker rouge, 'what you have there is too light.' Stupefied, O teased her nipples with her fingertips until she felt them harden and prick up; she hid them with the palms of her hands. 'No,' said Sir Stephen, 'don't.' She removed her hands and lay back in the couch: her breasts were heavy for so slender a torso, and as she reclined, their weight dragged them on to one side, one to the other, towards her armpits. What was preventing Sir Stephen from approaching his mouth, why did he not advance his hand towards the nipples he had wished to see stiffen and which she felt tremble with each breath she drew, still though she was? But he had come near. He was sitting on the arm at the end of the couch. But he had come no nearer, he wasn't touching her. He was smoking. His hand twitched – O never knew whether that movement was voluntary or not – but, in twitching it, caused a flick of hot ash to fall between her breasts. She had the feeling he wished to insult her, it was as disdaining she interpreted his silence, the quality of detachment in his attention, his inattention. However, he had desired her shortly before, he still did desire her now, she could tell it by the straining bulge under his robe's loosewoven cloth. Oh, then let him take her,

67

even if it were to hurt her! She detested her own desire, she detested Sir Stephen for the control he was exerting over himself. She wanted him to love her, there was the truth: wanted him to be impatient to touch her lips, to penetrate her body; let him then shake her to her depths, lay her waste, but not maintain this calm in face of her, and not impose this terrible restraint upon his pleasure. It had made not the slightest difference to her whether, at Roissy, those who used her had in doing so felt anything at all: they were the instruments by means of whom her lover extracted pleasure from her, by means of whom she became what he wanted her to be, as smooth and cool as a pebble in a brook. Their hands had been his hands, their orders his orders. But not now, not here. René had turned her over to Sir Stephen, but it was very plain that he wanted to share her with him, not in order to obtain more from her, but to share with Sir Stephen what at the present time he cherished most, when in past days, when they were younger, they had shared a journey together, or a boat, or a horse. And this present sharing derived its meaning much more from René's relation to Sir Stephen than from René's to her. That which each of the two was going to seek in her would be the mark of the other, the trace of the other's passage. A little while ago, when she had been kneeling half-naked against René, and when Sir Stephen had opened her legs with both hands, René had explained how O's anus had become so distended, and why he had been delighted to see it being stretched: he had at the time thought of how much Sir Stephen would enjoy having the hole he preferred always ready, always available, always easy; and René had even gone on to say, that if Sir Stephen liked, he, René would leave its use entirely to him, Sir Stephen. 'Why, gladly, that's very nice,' Sir Stephen had said, but he had remarked that, stretched though it did appear to have been, there was some danger that he tear O, to a certain degree. 'O belongs to you,' René had replied immediately, 'O will be happy to be torn to a certain degree.' And he had bent towards her and kissed her hands. The mere idea that René could thus imagine depriving himself of some part of her had left O thunderstruck. In it, she had per-

ceived the indication perhaps of a tendency: that she meant
less to her lover than did Sir Stephen. And also, although he
had so often told her that in her he loved the object he had
made of her, the absolute disposition of her he enjoyed, the
freedom that was his to do with her what he wished, as one is
free to dispose of a piece of furniture which one takes as much
and sometimes more pleasure in giving away than in keeping
for oneself, she realized now that she had not entirely believed
him then. She saw yet another indication, this time of what
one could hardly call deference towards Sir Stephen, in the
fact that René, who so passionately loved to see her under
the bodies or blows of others than he, who with such devoted
tenderness, with such unwaring gratitude, would watch her
mouth open to emit moans of pleasure or screams, watch her
eyes open wide, wide with pain or shut tight over tears, had
left her after making sure, in exposing her, in opening her
secret parts the way one opens the mouth of a horse and ex-
hibits the teeth to show that the animal is young enough, that
Sir Stephen found her young enough, pretty enough or at least
suitable for his own purposes and was willing to accept her.
This behaviour, outraging, perhaps, perhaps outrageous, changed nothing in O's love for René. She considered herself fortunate, was happy to find that she was important enough to
him to enable him to find pleasure in outraging her, as be-
lievers thank God for having humbled them. But in Sir Stephen
she divined a glacial unswerving will which desire was power-
less to deflect from its purpose and before which, up until
now, exciting as she might be, submissive as she certainly was,
she counted for absolutely nothing. Otherwise why would she
have experienced such fear? The scourge tucked in the Roissy
valets' belts, the virtually constantly worn chains had seemed
less dreadful to her than the equanimity in the gaze Sir Stephen
trained upon her breasts, upon breasts he did not touch. Upon
her little shoulders she could feel their slight weight; smooth
and inflated, their slight weight weighed nevertheless upon her
little chest; she knew how fragile they were. She could not
make them stop trembling, to do that she would have had to
have stopped breathing. To hope that that fragility would dis-

arm Sir Stephen was futile, and she knew very well that, quite the other way, her passively offered sweetness, her helplessness beckoned to wounds as much as to caresses, to fingernails as much as to lips. She underwent an instant of illusion: Sir Stephen's right hand, the one holding his cigarette, grazed their nipples, his middle finger grazed those nipples, which responded by stiffening further. What was this for Sir Stephen? some sort of game and no more, some sort of procedure of verification, such as one might employ to test the excellence and proper functioning of a mechanism? She was in no doubt as to the answer. Still perched on the arm of the couch, Sir Stephen then told her to get rid of her skirt. The fastening clasps didn't readily unfasten under O's sweating, shaking fingers, she required two attempts before she succeeded in getting out of the black faille half-slip under her skirt. When she was at length completely naked, her shiny high-heeled slippers and her rolled-down black nylon stockings emphasizing the slender lines of her legs and the whiteness of her thighs, Sir Stephen, who had also risen, grasped her womb with the spread fingers of one hand and thrust her towards the couch. He made her kneel, her back against the couch, and so as to make her lean more of her weight against her shoulders, he had her spread her thighs a little. This brought her waist forward, away from the couch. Her hands lay by her ankles. Her sex gaped. Above her defenseless breasts was her exposed throat, for she had flung back her head. She didn't dare look at Sir Stephen's face, but, from the corner of her eye, she saw his hands unknot the belt of his dressing-gown. When he had approached her, was standing straddling her, when he had seized her by the nape, then he stuffed himself into her mouth. It wasn't the caress of her lips all along the length of his member, it wasn't that he was seeking, but rather the depths of her throat he was aiming at. He thrust, thrust again, pushed for a long time, and O felt the gag of flesh swell and harden until it choked her, and still he thrust, and the repeated coming and going brought tears to her eyes. The better to invade her, Sir Stephen had knelt on the couch, one knee on either side of O's face, and there were instants when his buttocks rested on O's breasts, and she felt

70

her womb, useless and scorned, burn. Despite the great length of time he spent in her mouth, Sir Stephen did not bring his pleasure to a climax, but finally withdrew from her in silence, stood up, and closed his dressing-gown. 'You,' he said. 'You are easy, O. Wanton, one might say. You love René, but you are wanton. I wonder whether René realizes it. Is he aware that you yearn for every one of the men who desire you? Is he aware that in sending you to Roissy or in giving you to others he is simply providing you with ready-made alibis for your own wantonness?'

'I love René,' O replied.

'Do you? I dare say you do. You love René, but you yearn for others. Myself, for example,' Sir Stephen said.

Yes, she wanted him; but if she were to say so, and if René were to hear of it, would he change? She didn't know; all she could do was keep still and lower her eyes: to have gazed at Sir Stephen would have been tantamount to a confession. Then Sir Stephen approached and, taking her by the shoulders, made her lie down upon the carpet: she found herself on her back, her legs drawn up, her knees flexed. Sir Stephen had seated himself on the same spot where, a moment ago, she had been leaning upon the couch; he caught her right knee and dragged her to him. As she was squarely opposite the fire-place, the nearby fire shed an intense light upon the two well-opened cracks of her womb and her behind. Without letting go of her, Sir Stephen curtly bade her caress herself, but not to close her legs back together. Numb, she obediently stretched her right hand down towards her sex and her fingers encountered, between the already parted fleece, the already burning morsel of flesh placed above where the fragile lips of her sex joined together. She touched that morsel of flesh, then her hand fell away, she stammered: 'I can't.' And she actually could not. She had never caressed herself except furtively, in the warmth and covering obscurity of her bed, when she had been alone; and never had she pursued her pleasure through to a crisis. She'd stopped, gone to sleep, sometimes found the crisis in an ensuing dream, and had waked, disappointed that it had been simultaneously so strong and so transitory. Sir

Stephen's stare was obstinate, compelling. She couldn't withstand it and, repeating her 'I can't,' shut her eyes. For she saw it again, and couldn't get it out of her head, and every time she saw it she had the same nauseous sensation she'd had when she'd actually witnessed it when she was fifteen years old: Marion slumped in a leather armchair in a hotel room, Marion, one leg flung over an arm of the chair and her head sagging down towards the other arm: caressing herself, and moaning, in front of O. Marion had told her that she'd once caressed herself that way in the office where she worked and at a time when she thought there was no one else there; and the boss had suddenly walked in and caught her smack redhanded in the middle of the act. O had a recollection of Marion's office: a room, a bare room, pale green walls, light coming in from the North through dusty windows. One chair in the room, it was intended for visitors and was opposite the table. 'Did you run away?' O had asked. 'No,' Marion had replied, 'he asked me to go ahead and start again, but he'd locked the door and had made me take off my panties and he'd moved the chair over by the window.' O had been overwhelmed with admiration for what she'd considered Marion's courage, and with horror, and had shyly but stubbornly refused to caress herself in front of Marion, and had sworn that she'd never caress herself in front of anyone else. Marion had laughed and said: 'You'll see when your lover asks you to.' René had never asked her to. Would she have done it had he asked? Of course she would have, but terrified lest she see dawn in René's eyes the same look of disgust she herself had felt while watching Marion. Which was absurd. And that it was Sir Stephen, that was still more absurd; what difference did it make to her if Sir Stephen were disgusted? But no, she couldn't. For the third time, she murmured: 'I can't.' Low as was the voice in which it was spoken, he heard it, released her, rose, tied his robe shut, ordered O to get up. 'That – am I to take that for obedience?' he asked. Then he trapped her two wrists in his left hand, swung his right hand back and slapped her hard. She wavered, staggered, would have fallen had he not held her upright. 'Kneel down, I have something to say to you,' he said. 'I'm

72

afraid René has prepared you very poorly.' 'I always obey René,' she stammered. 'You fail to distinguish between love and obedience. You're going to obey me without loving me and without my loving you.' Thereupon she sensed a storm of revolt rise in her, a storm of the strangest revolt, silently and within her denying the words she had heard, denying the promises of submission and slavery she'd given, denying her own consent, her own desire, her nakedness, her sweat, her trembling legs, the circles round her eyes. She ground her teeth in rage and fought when, having whirled behind her, bent her spine forward till her elbows and forehead touched the floor, jammed his thighs behind hers and forced up her haunches, he drove himself into her anus, tearing her as René had said she would be glad to have him do. The first time, she did not scream. He went more brutally to work, and she screamed. And every time he withdrew, then plunged in again, every time, hence, that he wanted her to, she screamed. She screamed from loathing and revulsion as much as from pain, and he knew it. She knew it too, and knowing it was the measure of her defeat, she knew she was beaten and that it pleased him to force her to scream. When he was done and, after having jerked her to her feet, was on the point of sending her out the door, he advised her that what of himself he had left inside her was going to seep out gradually, to trickle out mixed with the blood from her gashed flesh, that this gash would go on burning her so long as her behind refused to accommodate itself to him, and that he was going to go on tearing it until it did. René, had he reserved to Sir Stephen this way of using her? Well, he heartily intended to take full advantage of René's generosity. He reminded her that she'd consented to be René's slave and his, but, he declared, it didn't appear to him as if she realized what she had involved herself in; no, in all likelihood she didn't. But she'd find out, and by the time he'd taught her it would be too late for her to escape. Listening to him, O told herself that, with the determined resistance she for her part heartily intended to put up, it would also perhaps be too late for him to avoid becoming enamoured of his work and end up loving her a little. For all her inward resistance and

73

the timid refusal she'd dared manifest had but one object: in some, however slight, degree, she wished to exist for Sir Stephen in the way she existed for René, and she wanted him to do somewhat more than desire her. Not that she was in love with him, but because she clearly saw that René loved Sir Stephen with the passion young boys have for grown-up boys, and because she sensed that, if need be and in order to satisfy Sir Stephen, he was prepared to sacrifice – if Sir Stephen were to require a sacrifice; a powerful intuition told her that René would align his attitude upon his, and that if Sir Stephen were to exhibit contempt for her, René no matter what his love for her, would be infected by that contempt as he had never been or even come near to being influenced by the attitudes of the men at Roissy. The point was that at Roissy, in regard to her, he'd been the master and the attitude of everyone to whom he gave her had depended upon his attitude. Here, René was no longer the master. Far from it. Sir Stephen was the master of René, whether or not René realized it; that is to say, René admired him, was striving to imitate him, to rival him, that's why he shared everything with him and why he'd given him O: this time, she had been really given, for good and all. It was as plain as day. In future, René's love for her would probably attune itself to how much or how little Sir Stephen reckoned she was worth bothering with and himself loved her. And so until Sir Stephen were to begin to love her, he would be her master and, regardless of what René might suppose, her only master in the strictest sense of the master-slave relationship. From him she expected no pity; but was there absolutely no hope of wresting some affection from him? Sprawled back in the big armchair by the fire René had occupied before departing, Sir Stephen had left her naked, standing in front of him, with instructions to await his further order. She'd waited without saying a word. Then he'd risen and told her to follow him. Still naked, wearing her high-heeled sandals and her black stockings only, she'd climbed after him up the stairway which began at the ground-floor landing, and they'd reached a small room, so small that there was space in it for only one bed, a dressing-table, and, between

74

the bed and the window, a single chair. This little room communicated with a larger one, Sir Stephen's, and both opened upon a common bathroom. O washed and wiped herself dry – spots of pink remained on the towel – removed her sandals and stockings, and got in between cold sheets. The window curtains were open, but the night outside was black. Before closing the intervening door, Sir Stephen approached her – she was already in bed – and kissed the tips of her fingers, as he'd done when she'd got down off the stool in the bar and when he'd complimented her upon her iron ring. And so he had been able to dig his hands and his sex into her, to ravage her behind and her mouth, but he did deign to touch his lips to her fingertips. O wept, and fell asleep towards dawn.

By noon the next day, O had been taken home by Sir Stephen's chauffeur. She had waked at ten, an old negress had brought her a cup of coffee, readied a bath and given her her clothing, all of it except for the fur wrap, the gloves and handbag which she later found on the drawing-room couch when she went downstairs. The drawing-room was empty, the curtains were open. Through the window opposite the couch, one could see a narrow garden, as green as an aquarium and planted in nothing but ivy, holly and spindle-trees. As she was putting on her wrap, the negress informed her that Sir Stephen had gone out and left a message: the woman handed her an envelope upon which only her initial was written; the white sheet of paper inside bore two lines: 'René telephoned to say he would fetch you at six at your studio'; after that, by way of signature, an S; and finally, at the bottom of the page, a postscript: 'The riding-crop upon your next visit.' O looked around the room: upon the table between the two armchairs, where Sir Stephen and René had been sitting the night before, there was, lying beside a bowl of yellow roses, a very long and very slender leather riding-crop. The domestic was waiting for her at the door, O dropped the letter in her bag, and left.

René, then, had telephoned to Sir Stephen, and not to her. Once home and after having taken off her clothes and lunched in her bathrobe, she had plenty of time to re-do her make-up and hair and dress again before setting out for the studio where she was due at three. The telephone didn't ring, René didn't call her. Why? What had Sir Stephen told him? What had they said about her? She remembered the words in which they had so casually discussed, from the point of view of their individual physical requirements, the advantages offered by her body. Maybe it was just that she wasn't used to this sort of vocabulary, but for these English terms the only French equivalents she could find were perfectly foul. True, she had been as much handled and fingered as any prostitute in any brothel; and so why shouldn't she be called a whore? 'I love you, René, I love you,' she repeated, whispering to him in the solitude of her room, 'I love you, do what you want with me, but don't leave me, my God don't leave me.'

What pity is there for those who wait? They are so immediately recognizable: by their dulcet aspect, by their falsely attentive stare – attentive, yes, but their attention is fixed elsewhere than upon what meets their stare – by their absent-mindedness, their absence are they known. In the studio she had a little plump red-headed mannequin posing hats, she didn't know the girl; for three whole hours O was that absent-minded person lured into forgetfulness by anguish, by the haste of flying time. Over a red silk blouse and petticoat she'd put a plaid skirt and a short suede jacket. The red blouse's brightness showing through her half-open jacket made her pale face paler, and the little red-head had said she looked like someone's *femme fatale*. 'Whose?' O wondered. Two years earlier, before she'd met René and loved him, she would have sworn: 'Sir Stephen's' and have said: 'he's going to know it, too.' But her love for René and René's love for her had robbed her of every last weapon, and instead of bringing her new proofs of her power, had deprived her of those she'd received up until then. Once upon a time she'd been indifferent and fickle, had amused herself tempting the boys who were wild about her, she'd tease them with a word, with a gesture, but never cede an inch, and if later she went to bed with them, she'd only do it once, just once, for fun and to reward them for having played the game, but also to inflame them further, and

76

to make crueller a passion she didn't share. She'd been sure
they loved her. One of them had attempted suicide; when he'd
come back cured from the hospital where he'd been taken, she
went to see him at his place, peeled off every stitch of clothing
and, forbidding him from laying a finger on her, lay down on
his divan. Ghostly white with desire and pain, he'd stared at
her for two hours, silent and petrified by the promise he'd
made. She'd never wanted to see him again. It wasn't at all that
she didn't take seriously the desire she aroused in him. She
took it seriously enough, for she understood it, or thought she
understood it, since she experienced an (as she thought), similar desire for her girl friends or for unknown young women.
Some of them yielded to her – those she'd then enticed into
overly-discreet hotels with narrow corridors and paper-thin partition walls – whilst others had backed off in horror from her
proposals. But what she fancied desire to be didn't go a great
deal further than the thirst for conquest, and neither her bad-
boy's manners, nor the fact she'd had a few lovers – if one
could call them lovers – nor her harshness, nor even her courage had been of the least service to her when she'd met René.
In the space of a week she became acquainted with fear, but
with certitude also, with anguish, but also with happiness.
René leapt at her throat like a corsair springing upon a captive, and, deliciously, she became captivated, at her wrists, at
her ankles, all over all her limbs and far down within her
heart's and body's secret recesses feeling tied by bonds subtler,
more invisible than the finest hair, stronger than the cables
wherewith the Lilliputians made Gulliver prisoner, bonds
her lover would tighten or loosen with a glance. She was no
longer free? Ah! thank God no, she wasn't any longer free.
But she was buoyant, a cloud-dwelling goddess, a swift-swim-
ming fish of the deeps, but deep-dwelling, forever doomed to
happiness. Doomed because those powerful ligatures, those
hairthin cables whose ends René held in his hand were the
only lines by which lifegiving energy could reach her. And
that was so true that when René slackened his grip upon her
– or when she fancied he had – when he seemed faraway, or
when he absented himself in what O took for indifference, or

77

when he remained some time without seeing her or answering her letters and when she thought he didn't want to see any more of her or was about to cease loving her, everything came to a halt in her, she languished, she asphyxiated. Green grass turned black, day ceased to be day, the night to be night, turning instead into infernal machines which made light alternate with darkness in order to torture her. Cool water made her nauseous. She felt like a pillar of salt, a statue of ash, bitter, useless and damned, like the salt statues of Gomorrah. For she was guilt-ridden, a sinner. Those who love God and whom God abandons in the darkness of the night, are guilty, they are sinners because they are abandoned. What sins have they committed? They search for them in their memory of the past. She would seek for them in hers. She would find nothing beyond silly little self-indulgences which derived more from her disposition than from anything she had done, vanities, trifling with the desires she'd awakened in other men than René, to whom she paid attention only insofar as the happiness René's love gave her, insofar as she was happy to belong to him, filled her with joy, and, abandoned as she was to him, that abandon made her invulnerable, irresponsible, and all her inconsequential acts . . . but what acts? For she could only reproach herself with thoughts and ephemeral temptations. Be that as it may, one thing was certain: that she was guilty, and that, without wanting to, René was punishing her for a sin he knew nothing of (for it was an entirely inner sin), but which Sir Stephen had detected instantly: her wantonness. O was happy René had had her whipped and prostituted because her impassioned submission would give her lover proof that she belonged to him, and also because the pain and the shame of the lash, and the outrage inflicted upon her by those who forced her to pleasure when they took her and at the same time delighted in their own pleasure without concerning themselves for hers, seemed to her to be the very absolution of her sin. There had been appalling couplings, hands which upon her breasts had been intolerable insults, mouths which had inhaled her lips and tongue like flaccid, repulsive bloodsucking leeches, and tongues and sexes, bestial and gummy and clinging, which, caressing her locked mouth, her desperately squeezed-shut belly-crack and behind, had electrified her with revolt, turned her so permanently stiff that it had been all the whip could do to unbend her, but to which blows had finally opened her, with an abominable and disgusting servility. And if, despite all that, Sir Stephen were right? If her abasement, her abjection were sweet to her? If so, then the baser, the viler she was, the more merciful was René to consent to make O the instrument of his pleasure. When she'd been a child she'd read a text written in letters of red upon the white wall of the room she'd spent two months living in, in Wales: a passage from the Bible, one such as Protestants inscribe in their houses: 'It is a terrible thing to fall into the hands of the living God.' No, she said to herself now, no, it isn't true. What is terrible is to be rejected by the hands of the living God. Every time René postponed the moment when they'd see one another, as he'd done that day – for it was after six, it was after six-thirty – O was brought thus to bay by the wolves of madness and despair; in vain. Madness all for nought, vain despair, there wasn't any truth any more anywhere. René arrived, he was there, he hadn't changed, he loved her, still loved her but he'd been kept overtime by a meeting or had had some additional work to attend to, he hadn't had a moment to call her up to say he'd be late. O, in a flash emerged from her veritable gas-chamber, and nevertheless each of these accesses of terror would leave a mute premonition behind, something that would stick in her depths, a warning of impending woe: for René'd neglected, or forgotten, to call her up, a round of golf or a bridge game had kept him overtime, perhaps some other face had held him up, for he loved O, but he was free, how free he was, and how sure of her, and casual, casual. A day of death and ashes, a day sandwiched between other days, but might not the day come that would justify the madness, a day when the gas-chamber's door wouldn't open in time? Ah! may the miracle last, may grace be not wanting unto me, oh René, don't leave me! O didn't see further, and refused to see further, than every day's tomorrow and every tomorrow's tomorrow, she refused to see beyond this week into next, and beyond next week into the one after that. And, for her, every night with René was a night forever.

René did finally arrive at seven; and he was so delighted to see her again that he kissed her squarely in front of the electrician who was fixing one of her flood-lights, in front of the little red-headed mannequin who was coming out of the powder-room, and in front of Jacqueline, who was expecting no one, and who suddenly entered the studio three steps behind the other model. 'Charming,' Jacqueline said to O, 'I was just passing by, thought I might ask you to let me see those shots we took. But I guess this isn't the moment, I'll try some other.' 'Why, Mademoiselle! that's quite all right,' said René, who didn't let go of O, whom he was holding by the waist; then, louder: 'Mademoiselle! Don't go, really.' O introduced them: Jacqueline, René; René, Jacqueline. Piqued, the red-head had vanished into the powder-room, the electrician was doing his best to look busy. O gazed at Jacqueline and sensed René gazing at her too. Jacqueline was in a ski-outfit, the sort only movie stars who don't ski ever wear. Her black sweater accentuated her small, well-separated breasts, her tapering black pants, her girl-from-the-land-of-snow's long legs. Everything about her suggested snow; the bluish sheen of her grey seal-skin jacket, that was snow under shadow, the wintery glint of her hair and eyelashes, snow in the sunshine. She was wearing a lipstick whose red bordered on purple, and when she smiled, and her eyes settled on O, O told herself that no one could possibly resist the desire to drink of those clear green and stirring waters under the frosty lashes, nor to rip off that sweater so as to lay hands on too-small breasts. There it was: René was no sooner by her side than, full of the certitude created by his presence, she recovered her taste for others, for herself and for everyone. They left the studio together, all three. Rue Royale, the snow that had been falling in huge flakes for two hours was still coming down, but now in little flakes, no longer soft, but hard, and they stung the face. The salt scattered on the sidewalks crunched underfoot and disintegrated the snow and O felt the icy breath of melting snow rise up beneath her skirt and fasten upon her naked thighs.

O had a fairly clear idea of what she was looking for in the young women she pursued. It wasn't at all that she was seeking to give herself the impression of being on a par with men, she wasn't trying, by means of masculine behaviour, to compensate for some female inferiority she didn't in the slightest feel. Oh yes, she'd once, at twenty, when she was courting one of her prettiest friends, surprised herself doffing her beret to say hello, standing back to allow her to go first, and offering a hand to help her get out of a taxi. Similarly, she wouldn't stand for not paying her share of the bill when she and a female friend went for some tea in a pastry-shop. She'd kiss her hand and her mouth too, if possible right in the middle of the street. But all that amounted simply to behaviour deliberately designed to shock, to the effects of childishness much more than to those of conviction. On the other hand, the strong liking she had for the sweetness of very sweet painted lips yielding to hers, for the enameled or pearly flash of eyes that half-close in the subdued light of divans at five o'clock in the afternoon when the curtains have been drawn and the lamp on the mantelpiece lit, for voices which say: oh, again, for God's sake, once again, for the well-nigh ineffacable marine odour which remained on her fingers, that liking was strong, it was real, and it was profound.

And keen too was the joy which she derived from hunting. It was probably not the hunting in itself, amusing or exciting as it could be, but the perfect freedom she felt thrill within her when she hunted. She controlled the game, and she alone (which, with a man, she never did unless it were on the sly). She held the initiative, the conversations, the rendezvous, the kisses depended upon her, even to the point where she preferred not to receive but to give the first kiss, and from the time she began to have lovers, she would just about never allow the girl she was caressing to caress her. The greater her yearning to see a friend naked before her eyes, the less she found any cause to take off her own clothes. Often, she contrived excuses to avoid undressing, said she was cold, that it was the wrong day of the month. Very few were the women, moreover, in whom she failed to find some element of beauty; she remembered the time when, just after having left school, she had wanted to seduce an ugly and ill-natured little girl simply because she had a wonderful mass of blond hair which in unevenly cut strands created a chiaroscuro upon a somewhat faded but fine-grained, smooth, absolutely matte skin. But the little girl had driven her away, and if pleasure had ever at any time lit her ungrateful face, it had not been out of thanks to O. For O loved, passionately loved, to see a face become transformed by that mist which renders faces so smooth and so youthful: a youthfulness which is outside of time, which is unrelated to it or to childhood, but which causes the lips to swell, makes the eyes larger as though by some artifice, and puts a clear scintillation into the iris. In this, admiration's role was more important than *amour-propre's*, for it wasn't her handiwork that moved O: at Roissy, she had experienced the same emotion before the transfigured visage of a girl being possessed by someone she did not know. Nakedness, the body's abandon had overwhelmed her, and it had seemed to her that her girl friends had bestowed upon her a gift for which she could never make a commensurate or equivalent return when they simply consented to exhibit themselves naked in a closed room. For vacation-time nudity, in the sunshine on the beach, left her quite cold – not at all because it was public, but because by being public and by not being unconditional it was, in some greater or lesser degree, protected. The beauty of other women, which with an unfailing generosity she had inclined to find superior to her own, did however reassure her regarding her own beauty, in which she saw (when one of her straying glances caught her reflection in some mirror), something like a reflection of theirs. The power she acknowledged her friends to have over her was, at the same time, the guarantee of her own power over men. And what she asked of women (and didn't repay them, save in such small measure), she was happy, and found entirely natural, that men imperiously demand of her. Thus was she simultaneously and at all time the accomplice of both women and men, and stood only to gain with each. Some people presented difficulties, the game wasn't always easy to win. That O was in love with Jacqueline, neither more nor less in love with her than she'd been with a lot of others, and admitting the phrase *in love with* was the right one (it was also a pretty strong one), there was no doubt whatsoever. But why didn't this love show?

When the buds opened on the quay-side poplars and when the daylight, slower now to die, allowed lovers time to go for walks in the public gardens after work in the office, she thought she'd mustered enough courage to tackle Jacqueline. In winter, Jacqueline had looked too triumphant in her cool furs, too enarmoured, untouchable, inaccessible. And had known it. Springtime put her in suits and low heels and sweaters, and gave her the appearance, with her short straight hair, of those impudent sixteen-year olds at the *lycée* whom O, a *lycéenne* too, had seized by the wrists and silently drawn into cloak-rooms and thrust against the massed coats. The coats would fall from the hooks and hangers, O would burst into wild laughter. They used to wear uniform blouses of raw cotton, their initials sewn in red cotton on their breast pockets. At an interval of three years and three kilometers away. Jacqueline had worn the same blouses in some other *lycée*; so she learned by chance when one day Jacqueline lay aside the dress she'd been modeling and with a sigh wondered whether, if you'd had clothes as pretty as these, you'd have been any happier at school. Or any happier if you'd been allowed to wear what they gave you to wear, but without anything underneath. 'What do you mean, without anything?' 'Without a dress, of course,' Jacqueline replied. Therewith O began to blush. She couldn't get used to being naked under her dress, and any even mildly equivocal remark seemed to her an allusion to her condition. In vain she reiterated to herself, that one is always naked under one's clothes. No, she felt as naked as the naked Italian woman of Verona who to save her besieged city went out to offer her self to the chief of the enemy: naked under a coat which one had simply to draw half an inch open. It also seemed to her that her nakedness was an atonement for something, a price she was paying, like the Italian woman, but for what? Jacqueline, being sure of herself, had nothing to atone for; she didn't need to be reassured, all she needed was a mirror.

O gazed at her with humility, thinking that the only thing one could properly offer her were magnolia flowers because their thick ripe petals blend softly into bistre when they fade, or perhaps camelias, because their waxen whiteness is sometimes alloyed by a pink glow. As winter retreated, the faint sunburn which gilded Jacqueline's skin disappeared with the recollection of snow. In a little while, only camelias would do. But O dreaded being laughed at, with these melodramatic flowers of hers. So one day she brought a great bouquet of blue hyacinths, whose heady odour is like that of sweet peas: an oily, heavy, cloying odour, full of everything camelias ought to have but don't. Jacqueline, who'd been wearing a pink lipstick for the last two weeks, buried her face in the stiff, warmly humid flowers. She asked: 'They're for me?' – asked it as do those women who are forever receiving gifts from everyone.

Then she said thank you, then she asked if René was going to come for O. 'Yes,' said O, 'he's going to come.' He's going to come, she repeated to herself, and it will be for him that Jacqueline, falsely still, falsely mute, will briefly raise her icewater eyes which never look one straight in the face. No one would ever need teach this woman anything: neither to be silent, nor to keep her hands still at her sides, nor to tip her head halfway back. O was dying to seize up a handful of the too-fair hair growing on that nape, to force that docile head all the way back, to trace the line of those eyebrows with at least a finger. But René would also want to. She knew full well why, once afraid of nothing, she had become so timorous, why she had been desiring Jacqueline for two long months without betraying that desire by so much as a word or a gesture, and was telling herself lies to explain this self-restraint. It wasn't true that Jacqueline was intangible. The obstacle was not in Jacqueline, it lay in O's own heart, and was so firmly planted there that she'd never had to cope with anything like it. It was that René was leaving her free, and that she abhorred this freedom. Her freedom was worse than any conceivable chain.

Her freedom was sundering her from René. Ten times over, without even opening her mouth to say a word, she could have grabbed Jacqueline by the shoulders, nailed her to the wall like a butterfly pinned to the table; and Jacqueline wouldn't have budged, nor perhaps have done anything but smile. But O was like one of those wild animals that have been taken into captivity and which act as the hunter's decoy or which down the quarry and which never leap save upon hearing the spoken command. It was rather she who, pale and trembling, sometimes sank back against a wall, nailed fast by her silence, leashed by her silence, and so terribly happy to be still. She was waiting for more than permission, for that she already had. She was waiting for an order. It came not from René, but from Sir Stephen.

With the passing of the months since the time René had given her to Sir Stephen, O came more and more to see, and with an increasing fright, the increasing importance the English man was assuming in the eyes of her lover. Simultaneously, it occurred to her that she was perhaps very mistaken, that she was perhaps imagining a development in the fact or in the sentiment where the only actual development was in the recognition of this fact or in the acknowledgement of this sentiment. Whatever the case may have been, she had been quick to notice that René was choosing those nights to spend with her, and only those nights, which followed the evenings when Sir Stephen summoned her to him (Sir Stephen keeping her the whole night only when René was absent from Paris). She had also noticed that when René remained present at one of these evenings, he never touched her unless to facilitate Sir Stephen's having of her and to maintain her at Sir Stephen's disposition if she struggled. Only very rarely did he stay, and never save at Sir Stephen's express request. At such times, as he had the initial time, he remained fully clothed, silent, lighting one cigarette after the other, chucking wood on the fire, refilling Sir Stephen's glass – but he himself wouldn't drink. O felt him watch her the way an animal-trainer keeps an eye on the animal he has trained, watchful to see that the animal, upon whose performance his honour is at stake, performs well; or

still more so, the way a prince's bodyguard, or a bandit chief-
tain's right-hand man watches the prostitute he has gone to
fetch out of the street for his master. Evidence that he was in
deed yielding to the vocation of a servant, or of an acolyte, existed in the fact he more closely watched Sir Stephen's face than
hers – and whenever he did glance at her, O felt herself robbed
of the very joy in which her features were drowning: for this
René humbly and admiringly and even gratefully owned himself indebted to Sir Stephen, who was responsible for creating
that joy, happy that Sir Stephen had consented to take pleasure
in something he had given him. Surely, everything would have
been much simpler had Sir Stephen been fond of boys, and O
had no doubt but that René, who wasn't fond of them, would
nevertheless have complied ardently, with the least and the most
trying of Sir Stephen's requests. But Sir Stephen was fond of
women only. She realized that through the agency of her mutu-
ally shared body they attained to something more mysterious
and perhaps more intense than an amorous communion, to a
union the very idea of which made her uneasy, but whereof she
could deny neither the reality nor the strength. However, why
was this sharing so to speak abstract? At Roissy, O had belonged, at the same instant, in the same place, to René and to
other men. Why in the presence of Sir Stephen did René ab-
stain, not only from taking her, but from issuing orders to her?
(He never went beyond transmitting Sir Stephen's). She put
the question flatly to him, knowing ahead of time what he
would reply. 'Out of respect,' René had replied. 'But I belong to you,' said O. 'You *first of all* belong to Sir Stephen.'
And it was true, true at least in the sense that when he had
abandoned her to his friend, René had abandoned her absolutely, and that Sir Stephen's least desires concerning her had
a priority over René's decisions or over his demands upon her.
Were René to decide that they'd dine together and go to the
theatre afterwards, and were Sir Stephen then to telephone to
him an hour before his appointment with O, René would
come to get her at the studio just as they'd agreed, but it would
be to transport her to Sir Stephen's door and to leave her there.
One time, but only once, O had besought René to ask Sir

Stephen to switch it to another day, so much did she wish to join René for an evening upon which they'd be alone together. René had refused. 'My dearest little one,' he'd said to her, 'haven't you finally understood that you don't belong to me any more and that the master whom you serve isn't me?' Not only had he refused, but he had communicated O's request to Sir Stephen, and in her presence had asked him to punish her so severely that she'd never again even conceive of shirking her obligations. 'Certainly,' Sir Stephen had replied. Adjoining the drawing-room was a little oval room with a parquet floor, where the only furniture was a mother-of-pearl encrusted table; it was here the scene took place. René didn't stay long: three minutes, all he needed to betray O and hear Sir Stephen's response, then he shook hands with the latter, smiled at O, and left. Through the window she saw him cross the courtyard; he walked straight out; she heard the car door slam, the motor start, and, in a little mirror niched in the wall, she glimpsed her own reflection: her face was white with despair and fear. Then, at the same moment she walked past Sir Stephen, who had opened the way for her into the drawing-room, she looked at him, mechanically: he was as pale as she. It came like an inspiration: the conviction shot through her, and immediately vanished, that he loved her. Although she didn't believe it, and derided herself for having imagined it, it comforted her and she undressed uncomplainingly when he gave her the signal. Then -- and it was for the first time since he had been having her come to him two or three times a week, gradually wearing her down, sometimes making her wait an entire hour, nude, before approaching her, listening to but never making any answer to her pleadings, for sometimes she pleaded with him, repeating the same injunctions at the same moments, as in a ritual to which he kept so strictly that she knew when her mouth was going to have to caress him and when, kneeling, her head buried in the silk of the couch, she was to offer him her behind only, which he was able, these days, to employ without tearing her, so wide open to him was she -- then, and it was for the first time, in spite of the fear that gripped her, in spite of the despair into which René's treachery had thrown her, she abandoned herself completely. And so mild were her consenting eyes when they met the burning pale blue eyes of Sir Stephen, that, for the first time, he spoke to her in French and in the familiar *tu* form:

'O, I'm going to put a gag in your mouth, for I'd like to whip you till you bleed. Will you allow me to?'

'I am yours,' said O. She was standing in the centre of the room, and her upraised arms, which a pair of Roissy bracelets on her wrists held aloft by means of a chain attached to a ring in the ceiling where there had once been a chandelier, made her breasts jut forward. Sir Stephen caressed them, then kissed them, then kissed her mouth, once, ten times. (He had never kissed her mouth before). And when he had applied the gag, which filled her mouth with the taste of wet cloth and which drove her tongue back towards her palate and upon which her teeth could scarcely take hold, he gently took hold of her hair. Swinging from the chain, she swayed on her bare feet, almost fell. 'Forgive me, O,' he murmured (he had never asked her forgiveness, not even her pardon), then he let go of her, and struck.

René did not return home to O's flat until past midnight after having gone alone to the party at which they had both been expected. He found her in bed, shivering in the white nylon of her loving nightgown. Sir Stephen had brought her back and put her to bed himself, and kissed her again before leaving. She told René that. She also told him she no longer had any desire not to obey Sir Stephen; saying this, she realized that René would surely conclude that she found it necessary, and agreeable, to be beaten, which was true (but there were other reasons as well). What she was beyond all else certain of was that it was equally necessary to René that she be. Great was his dread of beating her, so great that he'd never been able to bring himself to do it; no less great was his pleasure at seeing her struggle and at hearing her scream. Sir Stephen had, upon one sole occasion, used the crop on her in René's presence. René had pressed her down over the table and had held her still. Her skirt had slid down; he'd drawn it up again. It might be that he had a still greater need of the idea that while he was not with her, while he was off somewhere on a stroll, or working, O was twisting, groaning, sighing, weeping under the lash, begging to be spared and not having her prayers answered – and knowing that this suffering and this humiliation was being inflicted upon her by the will of the lover who loved her, and for the sake of his pleasure. At Roissy, he'd had her whipped by the valets. In Sir Stephen he had found the stern master he himself didn't know how to be. The fact that the man he admired most in the world could be pleased with her and could take the trouble to render her tame and meek, increased, O clearly saw, René's passion for her. All the mouths that had sounded her mouth, all the hands that had grasped her breasts and belly, all the sexes that had been sunk into her and which had so abundantly demonstrated her prostitution, had simultaneously demonstrated that she was worthy of prostitution and had in some sort hallowed her. But, in René's view, all that was nothing compared to the testimonial provided him by Sir Stephen. Each time she emerged from his embrace, René sought over her person for the mark of a god. O knew that if he had betrayed her several hours before, it had been to provoke the inscription of additional, crueller marks. She also knew that whilst the reasons for provoking them might disappear, Sir Stephen's for inflicting them would not. A pity. (But, secretly, she didn't consider it a pity, but the contrary.) Stunned, René stared for a very long time at that slender body upon which thick purple welts ran like ropes across shoulders, back, buttocks, belly and breasts, two welts sometimes intersecting. Here and there a drop or two of blood oozed through the skin. 'Ah, I love you,' he murmured. His hands trembling, he undressed, turned off the light and lay down beside O, close to her. She moaned in the darkness all the while he possessed her.

The welts on O's body took almost a month to go away, and at the end of this time there still remained, in those places where the skin had split, thin, rather whitish scars, like scars dating back to very long ago. But even had she been able to forget how she had got them, she would have been reminded again by the attitudes of René and Sir Stephen. Needless to say, René had a key to O's apartment. It had not occurred to him to give a duplicate to Sir Stephen, probably because, up until now, Sir Stephen had never evinced the desire to come to O's place. But the fact he'd brought her back that evening suddenly led René to suppose that Sir Stephen might consider this door, which only he and O could open, as an obstacle, as a barrier, as a limitation deliberately imposed by René, and it struck him as ludicrous to give Sir Stephen O if he didn't also give him free and unqualified access to her. In fine, he had a copy of the key made, delivered it to Sir Stephen, and only told O what he had done after Sir Stephen had accepted the key. She didn't think of protesting, and in her waiting for Sir Stephen's coming soon discovered an uncomprehensible serenity. She waited a good while, wondering whether he would surprise her in the middle of the night, whether he would take advantage of one of René's absences, whether he would come alone, whether indeed he would come at all. She didn't dare discuss it with René. One morning when by chance the cleaning woman wasn't there and when she'd got up earlier than usual, and when, towards ten o'clock, already dressed and ready to go out, she heard a key turn in the lock and rushed to the door, crying: 'René!' (for René would sometimes come in a little before noon, and she had been thinking of no one else), it was Sir Stephen, who smiled, and said to her:

'Fine, let's ring him up.'

But, obliged to stay on at his office because of a scheduled business appointment, René wouldn't be there for another hour. O, her heart beating wildly in her breast (and wondering why), watched Sir Stephen hang up the receiver. He had her sit down on the bed, took her head in his hands and opened her mouth to kiss her. Which he did, and for so long was she deprived of air that she might have slipped to the floor had he not been holding on to her. But he did keep her from slipping to the floor, and he made her sit erect again. She couldn't understand why such uneasiness, such distress was throttling her, for, after all, what could she possibly fear at Sir Stephen's hands that she hadn't already undergone? He asked her to remove

90

her clothes, and without a word watched her obey him. Could she have been any more accustomed to being naked in front of him, was she not equally accustomed to his silence, to awaiting the decisions of his pleasure? She was obliged to admit to herself that she'd been entertaining an illusion, and that if she was shaken by the place and the time, by the fact that, in this room, she had never been naked except for René, the essential reason for her anxiety was exactly what it always was: this state of being dispossessed of her own self. The only difference was that this dispossession had been brought home by the fact that she no longer had any space all to herself in a place where she had been wont to retreat in order to endure it, nor had she any night left to her, nor, consequently, any dream or any possibility of clandestine existence: no night to offset the length of the day as Roissy had offset the length of her life with René. That May morning's broad daylight made public what had formerly been secret: henceforth, the reality of the night and the reality of the day were going to be the same reality. Henceforth – and, O thought, at last. Here in all likelihood was the source of the strange security, mixed with fright, to which she felt she was abandoning herself and which she had somehow foreseen without understanding. Henceforth there would be no discontinuity, no gap, no dead time, no remission. He for whom one waits, because one awaits him, is already present, master already. Sir Stephen was a more demanding but a surer master, a safer one, than René. And however passionately O might love René, and he her, between the two of them there subsisted an equality, a parity (even were it but that of age), which nullified in her the feeling of obedience, the consciousness of submission. What he would ask of her she would also want immediately, solely because he asked it. But one would almost have thought that he had inoculated her with his own admiration for Sir Stephen, his own respect for him. She obeyed Sir Stephen's orders *qua* orders and was grateful to him for giving them to her. Regardless of whether he spoke English or French, addressed her as *tu* or *vous*, she never called him anything but Sir Stephen, quite as if she were not closely acquainted with him, or as if she were a servant. She told herself that the word

'Master' or 'My lord' would have been more suitable had she dared pronounce them just as it would have been appropriate if, speaking to her, he were to employ the word 'slave.' She also told herself that all was well, since René was happy to love her in the form of a slave to Sir Stephen. And so, her clothes neatly laid at the foot of the bed, having put her high-heeled slippers back on, facing Sir Stephen and her eyes lowered, she waited; he was standing over at the window. Brilliant sunshine poured through the dotted muslin curtains, strong rays of it fell upon her loins. O was not interested in striving for effects, but it did occur to her, right away, that she ought to have put on more perfume, that she hadn't painted the points of her breasts, and that it was great good fortune she had her slippers on, for the lacquer on her toenails was starting to chip. Then, of a sudden, she became aware of what she was actually waiting for, in this silence, in this flood of light, what she hadn't admitted to herself: that Sir Stephen gesture her or order her to kneel in front of him, undo his clothing and caress him. But no gesture, no order was forthcoming. From having thought the thought of her own accord, and alone, she turned scarlet, and all the while blushing thought herself ridiculous for blushing: what misplaced modesty, in a whore! It was just then that Sir Stephen invited her to sit down at her dressing-table and listen to him. The dressing-table wasn't a dressing-table properly speaking but, next to a ledge in the wall upon which were ranged bottles and brushes, a wide, low Restoration table and upon it a mirror where O, in her little armchair, could see all of herself. While speaking to her, Sir Stephen roved to and fro in the room behind her back; now and again his reflection moved across the mirror, behind O's reflection, but his image seemed faraway, for the silvering of the mirror was a bit fuzzy and the surface of the glass wavy. O, her hands limp and knees spread, would have liked to seize the reflection, make it halt in order to answer more easily. For, in the precisest English, Sir Stephen was putting question after question to her, the last questions O would ever have dreamt of hearing him put to her, if ever he would have put any at all. He had hardly begun, however, when he interrupted himself

92

and arranged O so that she was leaning back, almost lying in the chair; her left leg hooked over an arm of the chair, her right bent a little at the knee, in all that excess of light she offered herself and Sir Stephen a reflected view of her body as perfectly open as if an invisible lover had withdrawn from her and left her belly agape. Sir Stephen resumed his questioning, with a judge's firmness and the skill of a confessor. O not only saw him speak, she saw herself answer. Had she, since returning from Roissy, had she belonged to other men than René and himself? No. Had she desired to belong to others whom she might have met? No. Did she caress herself at night at such times as she was alone? No. Had she female friends by whom she might allow herself to be caressed, or whom she might caress? No (this no was more hesitant). But were there female friends whom she desired? Well, yes, Jacqueline, except that the word 'friend' would be overdoing it. Thereupon Sir Stephen asked her if she had any photographs of Jacqueline, for in describing Jacqueline as her 'companion', she had given Sir Stephen to understand that she had made Jacqueline's acquaintance at the studio. The photographs, however: he helped her get up to go and fetch them. René, out of breath after running up the four flights, found them in the living room: O standing before the large table upon which, bright black and white, shining like puddles of water in the night, were all the pictures of Jacqueline; Sir Stephen, half-seated on the edge of the table, taking them one by one as O handed them to him, and one by one setting them back on the table and, with his other hand, holding O's womb. As of that instant, Sir Stephen, who had said hello to René without letting go of her – she even felt him bury his fingers deeper in her – ceased to address her, addressed René instead. She clearly saw why: the understanding between the two men: René there, it reasserted itself: it was an understanding reached about her, but apart from her, she was simply its occasion or subject, there were no further questions to put to her, no further replies for her to make, what she was to do and even what she was to be was being decided over her head. Noon was approaching. The sun, falling vertically upon the table, was causing the prints to curl at the edge. O wanted to move them into the shade, to flatten them to prevent them from being spoiled; her hands fumbled, she was near to pleasure's critical point, so persistently did Sir Stephen's fingers probe her. She dropped the pictures, did indeed melt, moan, and found herself lying flat on her back across the table amidst the scattered photographs where Sir Stephen, having jerked his hand free, had thrust her, legs spread and dangling. Her feet didn't reach the floor, one of her slippers fell off, landed noiselessly on the white carpeted floor. Her face lay in the sun's path, she shut her eyes.

Much later, she was to remember, and when, much later, she remembered it, she wasn't struck by it, that she then overheard a dialogue between Sir Stephen and René as she lay there as if their exchange did not concern her, and at the same time as if assisting at an event she'd already lived through. And it was true that she had already experienced a similar scene; for when René had first taken her to Sir Stephen's, they'd discussed her in the same manner. But that first time Sir Stephen was unacquainted with her, and of the two, René had said the more. Since, Sir Stephen had broken her to the bit, familiarized her with all his fancies, had shaped her to fit him, and it was a matter of course, unthinkingly she had come to comply with his most outrageous demands. There was nothing left for her to cede; he had taken everything already. At least, so she believed. He was speaking, he who was in general silent when in her presence, and his words, like those René uttered in reply, indicated that they had returned to a subject which they often dealt with together, and it was she. The question was of what best to do with her, of how to get the most out of her, and to share what each had learned through his particular employment of her. Sir Stephen readily admitted that O was infinitely more exciting when her body was covered with marks, whatever their sort, if only because these marks prevented her from resorting to subterfuges and immediately proclaimed to whomever saw them that everything was permitted in her regard. For knowing it was one thing, visual proof, proof constantly renewed, was another. René, Sir Stephen said, had been right in desiring to have her whipped.

They decided that, quite apart from the pleasure her screams and tears might afford, she would be flogged as frequently as necessary, that is to say, the idea was to keep her marked at all times. Still on her back, her belly still afire, unstirring, O listened and it seemed to her that, by some strange substitution, Sir Stephen was speaking for her, in her place. It was as if he had been clad in her body, and as if he had experienced the anxiety, the anguish, the shame, but also the secret pride and the rending pleasure she experienced, particularly when she was alone in the midst of others, passers-by in the street, or when she got aboard a streetcar or bus, or when she found herself at the studio amidst the mannequins and the technicians, saying to herself that every single one of these people, if he were to meet some accident, if it were to be necessary to lay him out on the ground and call a doctor, would keep, even if unconscious, even if nude, his secret, but not she: her secret wasn't to be kept by her individual silence, its being kept or being known didn't depend exclusively upon her. Even if she wanted to, she couldn't indulge the slightest of her caprices — and that was just what one of Sir Stephen's questions had meant — without instantly divulging that secret, she could not undertake the most innocent of all possible activities, play tennis, or swim. It was good, it was sweet that these things were forbidden her, materially, as the grill in the convent materially prevents cloistered girls from belonging to each other and from escaping. For this additional reason, how could she take the chance of not being repulsed by Jacqueline without at the same time taking the risk of having to explain to Jacqueline, if not the truth, at least some part of the truth?

The sun had moved on and left her face. Her shoulders stuck to the glossy surface of the photographs she was lying upon, and against her knee she felt the rough touch of Sir Stephen's woollen jacket; he had approached her. René and he each took one of her hands and helped her to her feet. René retrieved her fallen slipper. It was time to get dressed. However, it was over lunch, at Saint-Cloud on the bank of the Seine, that Sir Stephen began to question her again. They were alone together. The tables spread with white cloths were distributed about a terrace bordered by a hedge and beds of dark red, newly-opened peonies. Even before Sir Stephen could make the sign, she'd raised her skirts as she sat down, and it had taken her bare thighs a long time to warm the iron chair. O heard the purling of the water as it moved against row-boats moored to a jetty of planks at the end of the esplanade. Sir Stephen was sitting opposite her, and O was speaking slowly, determined not to say one word that wasn't true. What Sir Stephen wanted to know was why Jacqueline pleased her. Well, that wasn't difficult to explain: it was because she was so beautiful, too beautiful for her, like the dolls, as big as they themselves, which are given as Christmas presents to poor children and which they never dare touch. And, at the same time, she knew very well that, if she'd never spoken to Jacqueline, never approached her, it was because she'd never really wanted to. Saying that, she raised her eyes, hitherto fixed on the peonies, and saw that Sir Stephen's were fixed on her lips. Was he listening to her, or had he only been paying attention to the sound of her voice, to the movements of her lips? She fell abruptly silent, and Sir Stephen's gaze rose and intercepted hers. What she read there this time was so clear, and it was so clear to him that she had read it, that it was now his turn to blench. If he loved her, would he forgive her for having noticed it? She could neither look away, nor smile, nor speak. If he loved her, how would things be changed? Had her life depended upon it, she would still not have been capable of a gesture, of fleeing, her knees wouldn't have carried her. He would probably never want anything from her but submission to his desire, so long as his desire lasted. But was desire sufficient to explain why, ever since the day René had given her to him, he had demanded her and kept her more and more often and sometimes simply to have her presence there and without asking her to do anything? Squarely in front of her, he was as silent and still as she; at a neighbouring table, some business men were holding a discussion while drinking coffee that was so rich and so strong that its aroma reached to where they were sitting; two Americans, smooth-faced, well-groomed and contemptuous, were lighting cigarettes in the middle of their meal; the gravel squeaked under the steps of the waiters, one of them came up to fill Sir Stephen's three-quarters empty glass, but why pour out wine to be drunk by a statue, by a sleepwalker? The waiter went away. Thrilled, O noticed that when his grey blazing gaze quit her eyes, it travelled down to fasten itself on her hands, on her breasts; then it returned to her eyes. Then, at last, she saw the shadow of a smile form upon his mouth, and she dared answer it. But speak, utter a single word? Impossible. She could scarcely breathe.

'O —' Sir Stephen said.

'Yes,' said O, in a very faint voice.

'O, what I wanted to talk to you about . . . It's already been decided by René. But also, I —' He broke off.

O never knew whether it was because, stunned, hallucinated, she had closed her eyes, or whether because he too was breathing with difficulty. He waited. The waiter changed the dishes, brought O the menu so that she could select a dessert. O handed the menu to Sir Stephen. A *soufflé*? Yes, a *soufflé*. That would require twenty minutes. Never mind, let it require twenty minutes, they'd have *soufflés*. The waiter went away.

'I need more than twenty minutes, though,' Sir Stephen said. And, in a steady voice, he continued, and what he said quickly proved to O that at least one thing was certain, that if he loved her, nothing was going to be changed on that account unless one could consider a change this curious respect, this fervour with which he was telling her: 'I'd be very happy if you'd like . . .' instead of simply inviting her to accede to his demands. Nevertheless, these were no more nor less than orders which there wasn't the slightest question of O's disobeying. She brought this to Sir Stephen's attention. He admitted it was true. 'But answer all the same,' he said.

'I will do what you like,' replied O, and the echo of what she'd just said rebounded in her memory: 'I will do what you like,' she had told René. She murmured: 'René . . .'

Sir Stephen nodded. 'He knows what I would like from you. Listen to me.' He was speaking in English now, in a low, muffled voice that was inaudible to the adjoining table. Whenever waiters approached, he ceased talking, when they'd moved away, picked up precisely where he'd left off. What he was saying seemed incredibly out of keeping with this public and peaceful place, and yet the most incredible of all was without doubt that he could say it and O hear it in such a natural manner. He began by reminding her that when she'd come to him that first evening he had given her an order which she hadn't obeyed, and further reminded her that, although he had slapped her then, he had never reiterated the same order since. Would she grant him from now onward what she had refused him then? O understood that it wasn't just that she had to acquiesce, but that he wanted to hear her say with her own mouth and in her own words that, yes, she would caress herself whenever he asked her to. She said it, and once again saw the yellow and grey drawing-room, René's departure, her revolt of that first evening, the fire glowing between her slack knees when she was lying naked on the carpet. That evening, in that same drawing-room ... But no, Sir Stephen didn't specify, and returned to what he had been saying. He also drew it to her attention that she had never, in his presence, been possessed by René (nor by anyone else), as she had been in René's presence by him (and, at Roissy, by a good many other men). From this she ought not to conclude that René would be the only one to inflict her with the humiliation of giving her to a man who didn't love her – and perhaps of finding pleasure in it – before someone else who loved her. (Vehemently, at length, pounding the words out, he assured her that she would soon open her belly and her behind and her mouth to those of his friends who might desire her when once they'd met her; and O was led to wonder whether this vehemence were not addressed as much to him as to her, and only the end of the sentence clung in her mind: before someone who loved her. What more could she ask for by way of an avowal?) Furthermore, he would himself take her back to Roissy in the course of the summer. Had she never wondered at the isolation in which first René, then he, Sir Stephen, maintained her? She saw no one else, only them, either together or separately. When Sir Stephen received guests in his rue de Poitiers house, he never invited O. Never had she lunched or dined at either that house or his apartment. Nor had

René ever introduced her to any of his friends save Sir Stephen. He would in all likelihood continue to keep her away from others, for Sir Stephen had the privilege of disposing of her. She need not however for one instant think that, while being his, she'd be less under private charter; to the contrary. (But what smote O's heart was that Sir Stephen was going to be with her as René had been, exactly, identically.) The ring of iron and gold she wore on her left hand – and, did she remember, that she had chosen so tight a ring that she'd had to force it over her finger? she'd not be able to remove it – was the sign she was a slave, but a common one, one held in common. It had been by mere chance that she'd met, since autumn, no Roissy affiliates who could have taken notice of her ring-symbolized servitude, of her irons, or manifested their recognition. The word *irons*, used in the plural, in which she had detected an ambiguity when Sir Stephen had said irons suited her so well, was not by any means an ambiguity, but a password. He'd not had to use the other formula, that is to say, whose irons are you wearing? But if the question were put to her today, what would she answer? O hesitated. 'To René and to you,' she said. 'No,' said Sir Stephen, 'to me. René's desire is that you first of all belong to me.' O knew it; why was she pretending that she didn't? In a little while, at any rate before returning to Roissy, she would have to accept a definitive mark which would not dispense her from common slavery, but which would designate her, among other things, as a particular individual's slave, as his, and next to which the traces left on her body by blows of a whip or a riding-crop, no matter how often repeated, would be unobtrusive and superfluous. (But what kind of a mark, in what was it to consist, in what way would it be definitive? Terrified, fascinated, O was dying from the need to know, and to know at once. But, apparently, Sir Stephen was not yet ready to explain. And it was true that she would have to consent, in the true sense of the word consent, for nothing would be forcibly inflicted upon her, she would have first to consent; she could refuse, nothing obliged her to remain a slave, nothing except her love and slavery itself. What prevented her from leaving, from getting completely out of this?) However, before this mark were imposed upon her, even before Sir Stephen were to make it a custom, as it had been decided between himself and René that he would, to so schedule her whippings that traces of them would be perpetually visible upon her body, she would be accorded a delay – time enough for her to induce Jacqueline to cede to him. At this point, stupefied, O looked up and stared at Sir Stephen. Why? Why Jacqueline? And if Sir Stephen was interested in Jacqueline, what had this to do with O?

'There are two reasons,' said Sir Stephen. 'Of these, the first and less important is that I desire to see you embrace and caress a woman.'

'But, how in heaven's name,' O exclaimed, 'how, even if we suppose that she were to take some liking to me, how am I to get her to consent to your presence?'

'There's nothing to it,' Sir Stephen said. 'Any way you like, by betrayal if necessary, and I am counting on you to get considerably more than that out of her. The second reason why I desire that she be yours is that you are to lead her – lure her, if you like – into going to Roissy.'

O tried to lay down the coffee cup she was holding in a hand which was trembling so violently that she ended up spilling the cups contents, dregs and a little sugar, over the tablecloth. As though scrutinizing the auspices, in the spreading brown stain she perceived appalling images: the horror-frozen eyes of a Jacqueline confronted by a valet Pierre, her flanks, doubtless as golden-hued as her breasts, haunches O had never seen but which now she imagined in an offered position and framed by her great red velvet robe, uplifted, tears streaming upon her downy cheeks and her painted mouth wide open and screaming, and her hair straight as straw falling down over her brow, ah no, it was impossible, not her, not Jacqueline.

'It can't be done,' she said.

'Yes it can,' Sir Stephen replied. 'Come now. How do you suppose girls are recruited for Roissy? Once you've brought her there, nothing more will be asked of you – and if she wants to leave, she'll leave. Come along.'

He had got suddenly up, leaving what the meal cost on the table. O followed him to the car, stepped in, sat down. They had only gone a little way into the Bois de Bioulogne when he veered off into a side road and parked in a little lane. He took her in his arms.

III

ANNE-MARIE AND THE RINGS

O had believed, or preferred to believe in order to give herself an excuse, that Jacqueline would be shy. She was disabused the moment she chose to be rid of an illusion. Jacqueline's modest airs – closing the door of the little room with the mirror where she put on and took off her dresses – were expressly calculated to intrigue O, to excite her desire to break down a door which, wide open, she couldn't make up her mind to go through. That O's decision was finally not her own but dictated to her by an outside authority, and did not result from this elementary stratagem, was of all things the furthest from Jacqueline's mind. This amused O at first. While aiding Jacqueline to re-do her hair, for example, when, having taken off the clothes she had been posing in, she put on her tight-necked sweater and the turquoise necklace whose stones matched the colour of her eyes, O found an extraordinary pleasure in thinking that Sir Stephen would, that same evening, obtain complete information regarding all of Jacqueline's reactions if she were to let her take hold of those two small, well-separated breasts on the other side of the black sweater, if her lowered eyelids were to lay those wonderfully light lashes on her cheek, if she were to. moan. When O kissed her, Jacqueline would become heavy, would be very still and as though expectant in her arms, would part her lips, toss her hair to one side. O had always to be careful to thrust her up against a doorway or against the edge of a table and to anchor her shoulders. Otherwise, Jacqueline would have slithered to the floor, her eyes shut, and without a sound. Directly O released her, she would turn back into something of frost and snow and tinkling laughter, distant, foreign, saying: 'You've got lipstick on me,' and wiping her mouth. This was the foreign, the distant person O loved to betray in taking such exact note – so as to forget nothing and to be able to relate it all – of the slow flush that would rise to the girl's cheeks, of the odour of sweat and sage about her. One couldn't very well say that Jacqueline was defensive or mistrustful. When she yielded to kisses – and, up until now, she hadn't granted O anything beyond kisses, letting herself be kissed but not kissing in her turn – she yielded all of a sudden, and one would have said completely, all of a sudden becoming someone else for the space of ten seconds, or five minutes. The rest of the time she was simultaneously provocative and coy and shy, incredibly skillful at parrying and evasions, never once failing to maintain a situation which, forever fluid, eliminated any possibility for a gesture or a word or even a glance which might have revealed the conquered one's conquest or allowed O to suppose that Jacqueline's besieged mouth wished only to surrender. The only indication by which one could be guided, and perhaps suspect the impending turbulence beneath the still waters of her gaze, was that occasional shadow of an involuntary smile, on her triangular face similar to a cat's smile, and, like a cat's, indecisive and fleeting, puzzling and disturbing. However, O was not long in remarking that two things could produce it, and that Jacqueline was aware of neither as a cause. First, the gifts she presented to her. The second thing was evidence displayed of the desire she aroused in someone – provided, though, that this someone who desired her might be useful to her, or flattered her. In what way, then, was O of use to her? Or could it be that Jacqueline simply found pleasure in being desired by O at once because the admiration O displayed for her was consoling or reassuring and also because a woman's desire can neither be dangerous nor have dangerous consequences? O was at any rate convinced that if, instead of bringing Jacqueline a mother-of-pearl clip or the latest Hermès scarf with I love you printed all over it in ninety-three languages, she had offered Jacqueline the ten or twenty thousand francs she constantly seemed to be short, Jacqueline would have stopped never having the time she never seemed to have to come for lunch or a bite at O's place, or stopped dodging her caresses. But O never had sure proof of it. No sooner had she spoken to Sir Stephen about what was going on – and heard his reproaches for allowing it to go so slowly – than René stepped in. The five or six times René had come for O at the studio and when Jacqueline had been there too, they'd all three gone out together either to Weber's, or to one of the English bars in the Madeleine neighbourhood; René would observe Jacqueline with precisely that same mixture of interest, of self-confidence and of insolence with which he'd looked at the girls who were at his disposition at Roissy. Insolence slid harmlessly and completely unnoticed off Jacqueline's glistening and stout armor. By a curious contradiction, those same darts found their mark in O, who viewed as insulting to Jacqueline an attitude she found perfectly correct and natural when shown to herself. Was she wanting to take Jacqueline's defense, or did she desire to be alone in possessing her? She really couldn't have told which, and all the more so in that she didn't possess Jacqueline – or not yet. But if she finally did succeed, it must be said that it was owing to René. Upon three occasions, leaving the bar where he'd had Jacqueline drink a good deal more whisky than she ought to have – her cheeks would become rosy, her eyes hard – he had dropped her off at her place before continuing with O to Sir Stephen's. Jacqueline lived in one of those sombre *pensions de famille* into which the White Russians had piled in the early days of the emigration and out of which they'd never subsequently stuck their noses. The vestibule was painted to resemble raw oak, the stairway's intricately turned balustrades were full of dust, clogged with grime, and great pale patches showed where the stair-carpeting had been worn on every step. Every time René – who'd never got past the front door – wanted to enter, Jacqueline, every time, shouted no, thanks a lot, and jumped out of the car and slammed the door of the house behind her as if some tongue of fire had suddenly shot forth and burned her. And indeed she was being pursued by fire, O would say to herself. She was to be admired for having guessed at what, so far, nothing could have enabled her to know. Jacqueline did at least seem to know that she had to be on her guard against René whose detachment appeared not to affect her at all (or was she affected by it? and insofar as being unaffected went, there were two involved in this game, and René could play it as well as she). That one time Jacqueline had let her enter the house and follow her up to her room, O had understood why she so adamantly refused to permit René into the place. What would have happened to her prestige, to the black-and-white legend on the slick pages of expensive style magazines, if someone other than a woman like O had ever discovered from out of what sordid den the glorious beast issued forth every morning? The bed was never made, the bedclothes were hardly even pulled up, the sheet one glimpsed was dingy and greasy, for Jacqueline never went to bed without massaging her face with cream and then went to sleep too quickly to think of wiping it off. A curtain must once upon a time have masked the bidet and the washstand, there now remained but two rings on a bent curtain-rod whence hung a couple of loose strings of cloth. The colour was faded out of everything, there was none left in the carpet nor in the wallpaper upon which the red and grey flowers hung on like some vegetation gone mad and become petrified upon a fake white trellis. You would have had to make a clean sweep, rip everything down, scrape the walls bare, throw out the carpet, scrape half an inch off the floor. But in any case get rid right away of those lines of filth which like stratifications striped the enamel of the washbowl, right away clean and put some order into the jars of make-up and make-up-remover, the pots, the bottles, wipe up the powder-box and the powder, sweep up the loose hair, throw away the dirty cotton swabs, and open the windows. But straight as a willow wand, as cool and clean as one and smelling of wild flowers, impeccable, spotless, unspottable, Jacqueline didn't give one small damn about her hovel. On the other hand, what she did give a big damn about and what weighed on her, was her family. It was because of the 'hovel', of which O had spoken to him in all frankness, that René made the suggestion to O which was to change their life but which when it had been framed as a proposal, Jacqueline

105

agreed to because of her family. The suggestion was that Jacqueline come to live with O. A family was hardly the word for it: this was a tribe, or rather a horde. Grandmother, aunt, mother, and even a servant, four women ranging in age between fifty and seventy, painted, yelling, smothered under their black silks and ornaments, sobbing at four in the morning in the cigarette smoke and little red glow of icons, four women in the click and clatter of glasses of tea and the pebbly hissing of a language Jacqueline would have given half her life to forget, she was going crazy from having to obey them, listen to them, and simply from having to see them. When she saw the way her mother could pop a lump of sugar into her mouth before taking a swallow of tea, she would set down her own glass, retreat to her dusty and dry little mop-closet, leaving the three of them, grandmother, mother, and mother's sister – all three dark with hair dyed black and eyebrows that met at the bridge of the nose, with great reproachful doe-eyes – in her mother's room which served as their salon and in which the servant ended up resembling them. She retreated, she fled, banging the doors behind her and behind her there'd come cries of 'Choura, Choura, little dove, little dove,' just as in Tolstoy's novels, for her name wasn't Jacqueline. Jacqueline was a professional name, a name for her job and for forgetting her real name and, along with her real name, this sordid and heartbreaking gyneceum, for getting a place in the sun, at least in the French world, in a more or less solid world where men exist who marry you and who don't disappear in mysterious expeditions like her father whom she'd never known, a Baltic sailor who had succumbed amidst the ice-floes of the pole. By way of family resemblance she had none save to him, she'd tell herself with rage and delight, to him whose hair and cheeks she had, and his bistre skin and slanting eyes. The one thing for which she felt grateful to her mother was for having given her that blond demon for a father whom the snow had reclaimed as earth reclaims other men. But she did not forgive her mother for having forgotten him to the point of one fine day giving birth to the issue of a short affair: a dark-skinned little girl, her half-sister by an unknown father, who had been named Natha-

106

lie, and who was now fifteen years old. Nathalie was to be seen only during vacation-time. Her father never. But he footed the bill for Nathalie's schooling in a *lycée* not far outside Paris, and to Nathalie's mother paid an allowance, not much, but enough to assure a mediocre existence in the idleness which was their paradise to the three women and to the servant – and even to Jacqueline, up until that particular day. What Jacqueline earned from her profession as a mannequin or, as they say in the American style, from her job as a model, when she didn't invest it in cosmetics or lingerie or in shoes bought at a top-notch shop or in outfits created by some top-notch *couturier* – she got them at a reduction, being in the business too, but, even reduced, the prices were still very steep – vanished into the family's privy purse, and further vanished into who knows where or what. Jacqueline could certainly have found a lover to keep her, and she hadn't lacked for occasions. She had accepted one or two lovers, less because they pleased her – they hadn't however displeased her – than to prove to herself that she was capable of inspiring desire and love. The only one of the two – the second – who was rich, had made her a present of a very handsome and somewhat pink pearl ring which she wore on her left hand, but she'd refused to live with him, and as he refused to marry her, she'd left him, with no very great regrets and relieved at not being pregnant (she'd thought she was, had lived in dread for several days). No, living with a lover, that was to lose face, to lose one's chances for a future, that would have been to do what her mother had done with the father of Nathalie, that was impossible. But with O, well, that was another story. A polite fiction would give the impression that Jacqueline was simply installing herself with a comrade, and sharing the place and costs with her. O would serve two purposes at the same time, would play two rôles: that of the lover who keeps alive or helps keep alive the girl he loves, and the theoretically contrary rôle of a moral caution. René's presence wasn't official enough to jeopardize the fiction. But in the background of Jacqueline's decision – who can say whether that same presence hadn't been the real motive for her acceptance? At any rate, it was up to O, and to no one else, to pay a visit to

Jacqueline's mother — she would have to ratify the agreement. Never before had O so keenly felt what it feels like to be a traitor, a spy, the envoy of a criminal organization, as when she found herself face to face with that woman who expressed heartfelt thanks for O's kindness to her daughter. At the same time, in the depths of her heart, O was saying no to her mission and to the reason she was there. Yes, Jacqueline would come to stay with her, but O would never be able, never, to carry obedience to Sir Stephen to the point of putting her into his clutches. And yet . . . For no sooner was Jacqueline established in the apartment — where, and it was upon René's request, she was given the room which he sometimes made a semblance of occupying (a bare semblance, in the light of the fact he always slept in O's big bed) — than O most unexpectedly found herself subject to a violent desire to possess Jacqueline at any price and if that were required in order to succeed, to surrender her to Sir Stephen. After all, she said to herself, Jacqueline's beauty was more than sufficient to protect her; and, she went on, why should I interfere? and if she is to be reduced to what I am reduced to, is that any great evil? This the while she fought not to admit (and yet trembled as she imagined), the immense joy she would have in seeing Jacqueline at her side, like her, naked and defenseless; like her.

In the course of the same week Jacqueline moved in, full permission having been given by her mother, René made a great to-do over the new situation, inviting both girls out to dinner and taking them to see films which, oddly, he selected from what was offered of detective thrillers, stories of drug-trafficking or white-slavery. He would sit between them, gently hold hands with them both, and say not a word. But during every violent scene O saw him glancing out of the corner of his eye at Jacqueline, watching for some sign of emotion on her face. It exhibited not much more than a trace of disgust which lowered the corners of her mouth. Then he would drive them home, and in the car, the convertible top down and the windows down, the night wind and the speed blew Jacqueline's thick blond hair down over her firm cheeks and over her little forehead and even into her eyes. She shook her head, flipping back her hair, would brush it back with her hand the way boys do. It being established that she was living at O's place and that O was René's mistress, Jacqueline, advancing from those premises, seemed to proceed logically to the conclusion that René's familiarities were perfectly natural. Without flinching a hair, she accepted the idea that René enter her room under the pretext that he'd left some document or other there, which, O knew, wasn't true, for she herself had emptied all the drawers of the tall Dutch secretary, with its flowery inlay and leather-surfaced hinged top always open, and which she'd always thought so out of keeping with René. Why did he have it? Why did he hang onto it? Where had he got it from? Its heavy elegance, its light contrasting woods were the only feature of luxury in the rather cheerless room which faced west, over the court, and whose walls were steel grey, and whose cold waxed wooden floor contrasted so sharply with the gay rooms giving on the quay. Fine. Jacqueline wouldn't like it in there. She'd all the more readily agree to share the two front rooms with O, to sleep with O, as she'd agreed the very first day to share the bathroom and the kitchen, the cosmetics, the perfumes and the meals. In all of this O was mistaken. Jacqueline was passionately attached to whatever belonged to her – to her rose-coloured pearl ring, for example – but absolutely indifferent to what wasn't hers. Lodged in a palace, she'd only have become interested in her surroundings if told that the palace belonged to her and if proof of ownership had been presented to her in the form of a notarized deed. Whether the grey room was agreeable or not, it was all the same to her, and it wasn't to escape from it that she came to sleep in O's bed. Nor to demonstrate to O a gratitude she didn't feel, but which, nevertheless, O ascribed to her, being at the same time delighted to abuse it, and she did think that she was abusing it. Jacqueline liked pleasure, and found it both agreeable and practical to receive it from a woman, in whose hands she ran no risks.

Five days after having unpacked her suitcases and with O's help arranged what had been in them, and when René had brought them home for the third time, towards ten o'clock, and had gone – for he had left, as he had the two times before – she

109

appeared in O's doorway, naked and still damp from her bath; she said: 'You're sure he won't come back?' and without even waiting for her answer, slipped into the big bed. She let herself be embraced and caressed, her eyes shut; she did not repay O in kind, she did nothing at all, at first she hardly reacted, hardly moaned, but then began to, then did moan louder and finally emitted a cry. She fell asleep, the light of the pink lamp falling on her face, her body stretched across the bed, knees apart, torso a bit to one side, hands open. The sweat glistened in the cleft between her breasts. O drew the covers over her, turned out the light. Two hours later, when she took Jacqueline again, in the darkness, Jacqueline submitted quietly, but murmured: 'Don't tire me out, I have to get up early tomorrow.'

This was the period when Jacqueline, in addition to her intermittent jobs as a model, took up the equally unsteady but more absorbing work of a bit-part player in movies. It was difficult to tell whether she was proud of being an actress or not, whether or not she saw these small rôles as the beginning of a career in which she might have wanted to make a name for herself. More with rage than with enthusiasm, she'd drag herself out of bed in the morning, take a shower and make up at top speed, swallowing nothing but the big cup of black coffee O would have just enough time to get ready for her; she'd give her fingertips to be kissed, put on a mechanical smile and glower with rancour: O was sweet and warm in her white bathrobe, her hair brushed, her face washed, with the air of someone about to go back for some more sleep. However, it wasn't true. O hadn't yet dared explain why to Jacqueline. The truth was that every day Jacqueline left the apartment, at the hour children set off for school and white-collar workers for their offices, O, who in the past had indeed spent most of the morning at home, would get dressed too: 'I'm sending my car,' Sir Stephen had said, 'the chauffeur will take Jacqueline to Boulogne and then come back and get you.' And O found herself arriving at Sir Stephen's every morning at an hour when the sun was still only striking the eastern façades; the other walls lay in the chill, but the shadows in gardens would be shortening. At the rue de Poitiers, morning tidying-up was still under way. Norah would conduct O to the little room where, the first evening, Sir Stephen had let her sleep and cry by herself, would wait until O had taken off her gloves and set them with her bag and clothes on the bed, then take them and, while O looked on, arrange them in a closet to which she had the key, then, having given O her high-heeled slippers which clacked when she walked, would precede her, opening one door after another for her until they came to the door to Sir Stephen's study, before which she would step aside to allow O to pass first. O never accustomed herself to these preparations, and taking off all her clothes before this patient old woman who seldom looked at her and never said anything to her was as much of an ordeal for her as being naked before the eyes of the Roissy valets. In felt slippers, the old negress drifted here and there in silence, like a nun. All the while she followed her, O could not take her eyes off the two points of her Madras headgear and, every time she opened a door, her thin brown hand, seemingly as hard as wood, on the porcelain doorknob. At the same time, coexistent with this awe she felt before Norah there was another, entirely opposite, but not, O thought, a contradictory feeling: she derived a certain pride from the fact that this servant of Sir Stephen (what, exactly, was her relation to Sir Stephen? his view of her? why had he entrusted her with this rôle, which she seemed so little suited for?) was witness that she too – like others, perhaps, whom she likewise guided about the apartment and attended to, who knows? – merited being utilized by Sir Stephen. For Sir Stephen – perhaps – was in love with her, yes, surely did love her, and O sensed that the moment was not far off when he was going, not just to let her think so, but to tell her so – but meanwhile, precisely insofar as his love for her and his desire of her remained at odds, his demands upon her were becoming ever more extensive, more exacting, more minute. Thus retained at his side for whole mornings during which he sometimes scarcely touched her, wishing only to be caressed by her, she accommodated herself to satisfy him with what cannot be called anything but gratitude, all the greater, that gratitude,

111

when his wishes would assume the form of an order. Each wish she surrendered to was her guarantee that another surrender would be required of her, each of his wishes she complied with was for her like some debt whereof she acquitted herself; how strange, that her indebtedness was immense; infinite; strange, perhaps, but it was immense, it was infinite. Sir Stephen's business office, located on the floor below the yellow and grey drawing-room he used in the evening, was less spacious and had a lower ceiling. Here there was neither canapé nor couch, only two Regency armchairs upholstered in flowered tapestry. Sometimes O sat down, but Sir Stephen generally preferred to have her nearer to him, within hand's reach, and while his attentions were absorbed in other matters, to have her sit on his desk, to his left. The desk was placed at right angles to the wall, O could lean her back against shelves containing dictionaries and leather-bound telephone books. The telephone was next to her left thigh, and she quivered every time the thing rang. It was she who would pick up the receiver and answer, asking: 'Who is it, please?' and repeating the caller's name aloud; she would then either put Sir Stephen on the wire or, depending upon what he signalled to her, explain that he was away or unable to take the call. When some visitor came, Norah announced him, Sir Stephen had the visitor wait long enough for Norah to be able to take O back to the room where she had undressed and where Norah came to fetch her again when, his visitor having left, Sir Stephen rang a bell. As Norah came in and out of the study several times every morning, whether to bring Sir Stephen coffee or the mail or to empty ashtrays, and since she alone had the right to enter there but also had instructions never to knock, and, finally, since when she had something to say, she always waited in silence for Sir Stephen to address her first and enquire what it was she wanted, it once came about that O was bent down on hands and knees upon the desk, her head and elbows resting on the leather top, her rump raised in the air, waiting to be penetrated by Sir Stephen, at the very moment Norah entered. O raised her head. Norah, who never looked at her, need not have now. But this time it was evident that Norah wanted to catch O's glance. The woman's hard, glittering eyes fastened upon her breasts, to which O had no way of knowing whether she was indifferent; those eyes in that deep-lined and expressionless face so startled O that she twitched, made an involuntary movement to escape from Sir Stephen. He understood; he pressed one hand down hard upon her back to prevent her from slipping away, and pried her open with the other. She who always made every effort to please was now, despite herself, tensely contracted, and Sir Stephen had to force his way into her. Even after he had done so, she felt the muscular ring squeeze tight around him, and he had considerable trouble thrusting himself the whole way in. He did not withdraw until he was able to move backward and forward without difficulty. Then, as he was about to take her again, he told Norah to wait and that she could dress O when he was finished with her. However, before sending her off, he kissed O upon the lips, and tenderly. It was thanks to that kiss that, several days later, she found the courage to tell him that Norah frightened her. 'I should hope so,' he said. 'And when you wear, as you shortly shall – if you consent – my mark and my irons, you'll have much better reason to fear her.' 'Why?' O asked. 'What mark? What irons? I already wear this ring –' 'All that is Anne-Marie's affair. I've promised to show you to her; shall we go to see her after lunch? She is one of my friends, and I suppose you've noticed that, up until now, I have never introduced you to any of them. When Anne-Marie is finished with you, I'll give you some very sound reasons for being afraid of Norah,' and, having heard that, O dared say no more.

She was intrigued even more by this Anne-Marie than by Norah. It was of her Sir Stephen had spoken during their outdoor lunch at Saint-Cloud. And it was indeed true that O knew none of Sir Stephen's friends, none of his acquaintances. All in all, shut up within her secret, she was living in Paris as though in a brothel; the only persons who had a right to her secret, René and Sir Stephen, at the same time had the right to her body. It occurred to her that the words *open oneself to some-one*, which signify to confide oneself, had, in their application to her, but one meaning: quite literal, physical, but neverthe-

　　　　　　　　113

less absolute and essential, for the fact was that she opened herself in every part of her body which could possibly open. It also seemed that there lay her *raison d'être*, and that, like René, Sir Stephen so construed her *raison d'être*, since when he spoke of his friends, as he had at Saint-Cloud, it was to tell her that those with whom he was going to make her acquainted would as a matter of course be entitled to the free use of her body if they had any desire for it. But, attempting to visualize Anne-Marie, and what in her, O's, behalf Sir Stephen expected of Anne-Marie, O had nothing at all to go on, not even her Roissy experience. Sir Stephen had also told her that he wanted to see her caress a woman – was this it? (But he had stipulated Jacqueline . . .) No, that wasn't it. He had just a moment ago employed the words 'to show you.' 'I've promised to show you to her' – that is what he'd said. And what did it mean? But when O left Anne-Marie she still did not know.

Anne-Marie lived near the Observatoire in an apartment flanked by a kind of large studio, on the uppermost storey of a new building from where one looked down over the tops of trees. She was a small, thin woman, Sir Stephen's age, and her black hair was streaked with grey. Her eyes were blue, but of such a deep blue that one could take them for dark. She offered Sir Stephen and O some very strong coffee in tiny cups: boiling hot, bitter coffee. It comforted O. When she had finished drinking it and had risen from her chair to lay her empty cup down on the table, Anne-Marie caught her by the wrist and, turning to Sir Stephen, asked: 'You'll allow me?' 'By all means,' Sir Stephen replied. Wherewith Anne-Marie, who until then, even upon greeting her visitors, even when Sir Stephen had presented O to her, had not uttered a word to her nor even smiled in her direction, now spoke in a very soft voice to O and smiled so warmly that one might have thought she was giving O a present: 'Come, my dear child, let me see you, front and back. But take off your clothes first, that will be much better.' While O was obeying, Anne-Marie lit herself a cigarette. Sir Stephen's eyes had not once left O. They left her standing there for some time, perhaps five minutes. There was no mirror in the room, but O caught a vague reflection of herself in the bright surface of a black lacquered firescreen. 'Take off your stockings,' Anne-Marie suddenly said. 'Look there, my dear,' she went on, 'look at your legs. You're going to spoil them by wearing those elastic garters,' and, pointing, she drew O's attention to the very faint crease which, a little above her knee, designated the place where O rolled her stockings flat around a broad band of elastic. 'Who told you to do that?' Before O could answer: 'The young chap who gave her to me, you know the one,' said Sir Stephen, 'René. But,' he added, 'he'll certainly concur in your view. Never fear.' 'Very well,' said Anne-Marie; and then, to O: 'I am going to give you some long dark stockings, and a corset to hold them up. But a stout corset. It will affect your waist-line.'

When she had rung and a blond, silent girl had come back with some fine sheer black stockings and a short corset of black nylon taffeta, held rigid by broad, very close-set whalebone battens curving inwards below the buttocks and round in front also, O, still standing, balancing awkwardly on one foot and then upon the other, drew on the stockings which mounted the full height of her thighs. The blonde girl helped her into the corset which buckled to one side and towards the rear. Also at the rear, as with the Roissy bodices, were laces to adjust the fit. O hooked her stockings in front and at the side by the four garter-snaps, then the girl set to lacing her up as tightly as possible. O felt her waist and belly dug into by the pressure of the battens which, in front, reached down almost to her pubis, leaving it free however, as it left free the entirety of her buttocks. 'She'll be much better,' said Anne-Marie, addressing Sir Stephen, 'when her waist is entirely reduced. Moreover, if you haven't the time to get her undressed, you'll not find the corset an inconvenience. Will you step this way, O.' The girl left the room, O went towards Anne-Marie who was sitting in a low chair covered with cerise velvet. Anne-Marie's hand strayed softly over her buttocks; then she had her bend down over a hassock – also covered with cerise velvet – raised her rump and spread her legs and, ordering her not to move, seized her two labia. This, O said to herself, is how they open the gills of fish at the market, and pull open the mouths of horses to show you the teeth. She also remembered that the valet Pierre, the first evening at Roissy, after he'd chained her, had done the same thing. But, after all, she was no longer her own, and what of hers belonged least of all to her was, very assuredly, that outer half of her body which could be put to use independently of her, as it were. Why then, every time she was made aware of it, was she not surprised at the discovery, but as though persuaded anew of the fact, why, every time, was she subject to the same distress which would paralyze her and which would put her much less entirely into the hands of him who took her than into those of whomever gave her to the use of some stranger, which, at Roissy, gave her to René when the others were possessing her, and here – to whom? To René, or to Sir Stephen? Ah, she no longer knew. But that was because she didn't want to know anymore, for it was very surely to Sir Stephen she belonged and had been belonging ever since – ever since when? Anne-Marie had her stand up and get dressed. 'You can bring her to me whenever you like,' she told Sir Stephen, 'I shall be at Samois' – Samois? O had been expecting to hear Roissy; but it wasn't Roissy, it wasn't that; what then was it all about? – 'in two days. That will be fine.' (What was going to be fine?) 'In ten days, if that suits you,' Sir Stephen replied, 'at the beginning of July.'

Sir Stephen remaining behind at Anne-Marie's, O, as she was being driven home, remembered the statue she'd seen as a child in the Luxembourg Gardens: a woman whose waist had been similarly compressed, a woman whose waist seemed so tiny midway between her heavy breasts and fleshy hips, that she'd been afraid the marble would snap in two ... and the stone woman had been bending forward, gazing at her reflection in a spring, also of marble and meticulously sculptured at her feet. Well, if Sir Stephen desired that ... Regarding Jacqueline, it would be very easy to tell her that all this was simply one of René's whims. Whereupon O was put in mind of an enduring thought she'd attempted to flee every time it came back to her, and which, nevertheless, she was always surprised to find less painful than it ought perhaps to have been: why, since Jacqueline had come to live with her, why had René

116

taken such care not only to leave her alone with Jacqueline, which could be understood, but to avoid being alone with her, O? July was approaching, René was to leave in July, he wouldn't come to see her at this place where Sir Stephen was sending her to be with Anne-Marie; was she therefore to have to resign herself to not seeing him except on those evenings when it pleased him to invite Jacqueline and her out, or – and she didn't know what, as of that moment, was the most upsetting (since between the two of them there remained nothing beyond these essentially false relations, false owing to the fact that they were limited) – sometimes during the morning when she was with Sir Stephen and when Norah first announced his arrival and then ushered him in? Sir Stephen received regular visits from him, René regularly kissed O, caressed the points of her breasts, with Sir Stephen formed plans for the next day, plans which did not involve her, and then left. Had he so thoroughly given her to Sir Stephen that he had reached the stage of not loving her anymore? What was going to happen if he didn't love her anymore? O was gripped by such a panic that she got out unthinkingly upon the quay in front of her house and, instead of getting back into the car, dashed off to find a taxi. There aren't many taxis on the quai de Béthune. She ran all the way to the Boulevard Saint-Germain and then had to wait some more. She was in a sweat, all out of breath, for her corset was impeding her respiration, and then at last a taxi did slow down at the rue du Cardinal-Lemoine corner. She waved at the driver, he drew up, she gave him the address of the office where René worked, got in, without knowing whether René would be there, whether he'd be able to see her, whether he'd want to if he was there, she'd never been there before. She was surprised neither by the tall building in a street leading off the Champs-Elysées, nor by the American-style office-rooms, but the attitude of René, who did have her come in right away, disconcerted her. Not that he was aggressive, or full of reproaches. She would have preferred reproaches, for, after all, he'd not given her permission to break in upon him that way, it was, after all, a disturbance, perhaps a considerable disturbance to him. He sent his secretary out, asked her

117

not to let anyone in nor, if any telephone call came, to connect him. Then he asked O what the matter was. 'I was afraid, oh, I was dreadfully afraid that you don't love me anymore,' said O. He laughed.

'All of a sudden, just out of a clear sky?'

'Yes, in the car coming back ... back from –'

'From whom?'

O said nothing. René laughed once again.

'But,' he said, 'I know. Silly thing.' He laughed. 'From Anne-Marie's apartment. And you're going to Samois in ten days. Sir Stephen's just phoned me.'

René was sitting in the only comfortable chair in his office, he was facing the table, and O was huddled in his arms. 'What they do to me ... I don't care what they do,' she murmured, 'as long as you love me. Tell me you still do.'

'My sweetest little creature,' he said, 'I do love you, but I want you to obey me and you don't, or not well. You've told Jacqueline that you belong to Sir Stephen, you've talked to her about Roissy?' O assured him that she hadn't. Jacqueline accepted her caresses, but the day she knew that O ... René prevented her from finishing her sentence, lifted her up, leaned her against the chair he'd just got up from, then raised her skirt. 'Ah, ha, there's the corset,' he mused. 'It's true, you'll be much more attractive when your waist is trimmed down.' Then he took her, and it struck O that it had been such a long time since he'd done it that, deep down inside her, she noticed, she had even doubted whether he still wanted her, and in this she found a proof of his love. 'You know,' he said to her afterwards, 'you are stupid not to talk to Jacqueline. We need her at Roissy, the best and easiest way would be for you to lead her there. But you hesitate; well, perhaps it doesn't matter. When you come back from Samois your true condition will speak for itself, you'll no longer be able to hide anything from her.' O asked why. 'You'll see,' said René. 'You've still five days to go, only five, for five days before he sends you to Anne-Marie, Sir Stephen intends to begin whipping you again every day, day in and day out, and you'll certainly show traces of it, and how will you explain them to Jacqueline? How? I wonder.' O did not reply. What René didn't know was that Jacqueline was interested in her only because of O's passion for her, and otherwise never even glanced at her. If she were to be covered with welts, she'd have only to be careful not to bathe while Jacqueline was there, and to wear a nightgown. She hadn't noticed that O wasn't wearing panties, she wouldn't notice anything: O didn't interest her. 'Listen,' René said, 'there is at any rate one thing you're going to tell her and tell her right away: that I'm in love with her.' 'And is it true?' O asked. 'I want to have her,' said René, 'and since you can't or won't do anything, I'll do what has to be done myself.' 'Roissy – she'd never agree,' said O. 'No? Well then,' René said, 'she'll end up landing there by force.'

That same evening, night having fallen, Jacqueline being in bed and O having drawn back the sheet to look at her by the light of the lamp, after having told her that 'René is in love with you' – for O told her that, and told it to her at once – O, who at the idea of seeing this so fragile and slender body belaboured by the lash, of this tight sex wrenched open, this pure mouth howling and the down on those cheeks sticky from tears, had, a month earlier, been horrified, repeated René's last remark to herself, and was happy.

Jacqueline gone and probably not to get back until the beginning of August if the film she was working in were to be completed by then, nothing remained to keep O in Paris. July was around the corner, all the gardens were a crimson riot of geraniums, all the awnings were lowered against the noonday glare, René was sighing that he couldn't get out of having to make a trip to Scotland. There was a moment when O had hopes he'd take her along with him. But apart from the fact that he never took her to see his family, she knew that he would yield her to Sir Stephen if Sir Stephen demanded her. Sir Stephen declared that he would come to get her the day René took the plane for London. Her work had stopped for the summer holiday. 'We are going to the home of Anne-Marie,' said he, 'she expects you. Don't bother about luggage, you shan't need anything.' They went to see Anne-Marie – not to the Observatoire apartment where they'd first met, but to a little cottage at the end of a big garden, situated on the edge of the forest of Fontainebleau. Since the day it had been given to her, O had everyday worn the whaleboned corset which Anne-Marie had esteemed so necessary: with each passing day, she laced it tighter, and by now one could almost circle O's waist with one's ten fingers: Anne-Marie would be satisfied. When they arrived it was two in the afternoon, the house seemed asleep, and in answer to the doorbell, the dog barked feebly: a big shaggy collie who sniffed O's knees under her skirt. Anne-Marie was reclining on a chaise-longue under a purple beech at the far end of the lawn which, in an angle in the garden, faced the windows of her bedroom. She didn't get up. 'Here's O,' said Sir Stephen, 'you know what's to be done, when will she be ready?' Anne-Marie gazed at O. 'You haven't told her about the operation? No? Well, I might as well start right now. One ought to count on ten days. I suppose you want to put the rings and the mark on in person? You do? Come back in two weeks. Then everything should be in order two weeks after that.' O wanted to say something, to ask a question. 'One moment, O,' said Anne-Marie, 'go to your room, it's in front, undress yourself. Leave your sandals on. Then come back here.' The room was empty, a big white room with heavy violet curtains. O put her bag, her gloves, her clothes upon a little chair near the door of a closet. There was no mirror. She re-emerged slowly, dazzled by the sun before regaining the shade of the beech. Sir Stephen was still standing in front of Anne-Marie, she was still lying down, the dog curled up at her feet. Anne-Marie's black and grey hair shone as if oiled, her blue eyes looked black. She was dressed in white, had a patent-leather belt round her waist, and was wearing patent-leather sandals, her toenails were painted the same colour as her fingernails. 'O,' she said, 'kneel before Sir Stephen.' O knelt, her hands behind her back, her nipples trembling. The dog looked as though he were about to spring upon her. 'Here, Turk,' said Anne-Marie. 'O, do you consent to wear the rings and the insignia Sir Stephen desires to have you wear, without knowing beforehand how they will be put upon you?' 'Yes,' said O. 'Then I shall see Sir Stephen to his car. Stay there.'

Sir Stephen bent and took O's breasts in his hands while Anne-Marie was getting up from her chaise-longue. He kissed her upon the mouth, murmured: 'You are mine. O, you are really mine?' and then he left her to follow Anne-Marie. The gate banged, Anne-Marie returned. O was sitting back on her heels and had laid her hands upon her knees, like an Egyptian statue.

Three other girls lived in the house, each of them had a room on the second floor; the one O was assigned to was on the ground floor, next to Anne-Marie's. Anne-Marie called to the girls, shouting to them to come down to the garden. All three, like O, were naked. In this house of women, carefully hidden by the high walls of the park and, on the side facing a dirt lane, by shuttered windows, only Anne-Marie and her servants wore clothing: a cook and two housemaids, older than Anne-Marie, severe in their black alpaca skirts and starched aprons. 'Her name is O,' said Anne-Marie, who had resumed her place on the couch. 'Bring her here, I want to have a closer look at her.' Two of the girls – both brunettes, their hair as dark as the fleece on their sexes, their nipples long and almost violet – helped O to her feet. The other girl was small, chubby, had red hair, and below the somewhat chalky skin on her chest showed a frightful network of greenish veins. The two girls pushed O almost on top of Anne-Marie who pointed a finger at the three dark zig-zagging stripes on the front of her thighs, welts which were repeated on her buttocks. 'Who whipped you?' she asked. 'Sir Stephen?' 'Yes,' said O. 'With what and when?' 'Three days ago, with a crop.' 'Beginning tomorrow, you'll not be whipped for a month. But you will be today, to designate your arrival, and as soon as I've finished examining you. Sir Stephen has never whipped the inside of your thighs, your legs spread wide apart? No? I dare say not. Men never know. Well, we'll attend to all that in due time. Now show me your waist. Ah, that's better, isn't it?' Anne-Marie kneaded O's smooth waist, pressed with her thumbs, then she sent the little red-head to fetch another corset, and then had it put on O. It too was made of black nylon, so stoutly whaleboned and so narrow that one would have called it a wide leather belt.

No garter straps were attached to it. One of the dark-haired girls laced it, and Anne-Marie ordered her to draw it as tight as she possibly could. 'This is terrible,' O said, 'it hurts terribly.' 'Exactly,' said Anne-Marie, 'and that is why you are much more lovely now. But you didn't tighten yours enough. From now on you'll wear this one this way, every day. Tell me now how Sir Stephen preferred to use you. I need to know.' She had gripped the fingers of one hand in O's womb, and O could not reply. Two of the girls had seated themselves on the ground, the third girl, one of the dark-haired ones, at the foot of Anne-Marie's chaise-longue. 'You,' she said, 'turn her around, let me see her behind.' O was turned around, her behind was presented to Anne-Marie, and the two girls pried it open. 'Of course,' Anne-Marie said, 'you've no need to reply. You'll have to be marked there, on the buttocks. Get up. We'll put on your bracelets. Colette will bring the box, we'll draw lots to see who's to do the whipping; Colette, go get the box and bring the disks. Then we'll go into the music room.' Colette was the taller of the two brunettes, the other was named Claire, the little red-head Yvonne. O had not hitherto noticed that they all three wore, as at Roissy, a leather collar and wristbands, and, as well similar bands at the ankles. When Yvonne had selected suitable bracelets for O and put them on her, Anne-Marie handed O four numbered metal disks, inviting her not to look at the numbers and to give one to each of them without looking at the numbers. O distributed the disks. Each of the three girls looked at hers, no one spoke, waiting for Anne-Marie to speak. 'I have two,' said Anne-Marie; 'who has one?' Colette had one. 'Take O away, she's yours.' Colette seized O's arms, brought her hands round behind her back, fastened the two wristbands together, and pushed her ahead of her. At the threshold of a French door which opened into a little wing forming an L with the main part of the building, Yvonne, who was preceding them, removed O's sandals. The French window admitted light into a room which, at the back, was a raised rotunda; the ceiling, a shallow cupola, was supported, at the entrance to the apse-like circular niche, by two slender columns spaced about two yards apart. On the floor of the niche was a platform, four steps led up to it, and like the rest of the room, it was covered with red felt carpeting. The walls were white, the French door curtains red, the curved divans rimming the inside of the niche were upholstered in the same red felt on the floor. In the rectangular part of the room, which was wider than it was deep, there was a fireplace and opposite this a large cabinet radio phonograph; to left and right, arranged in shelves, was a record library. This explained why the room was called the music room. By a door near the fireplace it communicated directly with Anne-Marie's bedroom. The symmetrical door, being unframed, resembled the door to a closet. Except for the divans and the radio phonograph, the room was bare of furniture. While Colette had O sit down on the edge of the platform – which, at the center, was more similar to a stage, the steps being to right and left of the columns – the two other girls closed the French door after having drawn the curtains about a third of the way. Surprised, O then noticed that it was a double door and Anne-Marie, who was laughing, said: 'Why, by all means, there's no reason to let the whole neighbourhood hear your screams. The walls, you will observe, are padded – nothing of what goes on here can be heard outside. Lie down.' She grasped her shoulders, thrust her down upon the red felt, then drew her a little way forward; O's hands clawed at the edge of the stage – she was about to fall – Yvonne fastened each of them to a ring, and her flanks were thus suspended over space. Anne-Marie made her double her knees up against her chest, then O felt her legs put under a sudden tension and drawn in the same direction: straps had been slipped through the eyes in her ankle-bands and hooked to other eyes half-way up the columns, she was drawn somewhat into the air and exposed in such a manner that the only visible parts of her were the cracks in her belly and behind, drawn violently open. Anne-Marie caressed the inside of her thighs. 'This is the part of the body where the skin is softest,' she said, 'don't spoil it, Colette. Go easy.' Colette was standing, straddling her waist, and through the bridge formed by her sunburned legs O saw the cords of the whip she was holding. At the first strokes, which burned her belly, O moaned. Colette, after striking to the right, shifted to the left, stopped, began again. O struggled with all her might, she believed that the straps were going to cut through her skin. She did not want to plead, she did not want to beg to be spared. But Anne-Marie intended to drive her to that, to begging and pleading. 'Faster,' she told Colette, 'and harder.' O's body stiffened, she braced herself, but in vain. A minute later she gave way to tears and screams, while Anne-Marie caressed her face. 'Just a little more,' she said, 'and then it will be all over. Just five minutes more. You can scream for five minutes, can't you? Surely. It's twenty-five past. Colette, you'll stop at half-past, when I tell you.' But O screamed no, no, for God's sake no, she couldn't bear it any longer, no, she couldn't stand this another second. However, she did have to stand it until the end and, at half-past, Anne-Marie smiled at her. Colette left the stage. 'Thank me,' Anne-Marie said to O, and O thanked her. She knew very well why Anne-Marie had judged it above all else necessary to have her whipped. That a woman was so cruel, and more implacable than a man, O had never once doubted. But O had thought that Anne-Marie was seeking less to manifest her power than to establish a complicity between O and herself. O had never understood, but had finally come to recognize as an undeniable and very meaningful truth, the contradictory but constant entanglement of her feelings and attitudes: she liked the idea of torture, when she underwent it she would have seen the earth go up in fire and smoke to escape it, when it was over with she was happy to have undergone it, and all the happier the crueller and more prolonged it had been. Anne-Marie had correctly calculated upon O's acquiescence and revolt, and knew very well that her pleadings for mercy had been genuine and her final thanks authentic. There was a third reason for what she had done, and she explained it to O. She felt it important to make each girl who entered her house and who thus entered an entirely feminine society sense that her condition as a woman would not lose its importance from the fact that, here, her only contacts would be with other women, but, to the contrary, would be increased, heightened, intensified. It was for this reason she required the girls to be naked at all times; the manner in which O had been flogged, as well as the position in which she had been tied, had the same purpose. Today, it would be O who would remain for the rest of the afternoon – for three more hours – with her legs spread and raised, exposed upon the platform and facing the garden. She would have the incessant desire to close her legs; it would be thwarted. Tomorrow, it would be Claire and Colette, or again Yvonne, whom O would watch in her turn. The process was far too gradual, far too minute (as, likewise, this manner of applying the whip), to be used at Roissy. But O would discover how effective it was. Apart from the rings and the insignia she would wear, upon her departure, and restored to Sir Stephen, she would find herself much more openly and profoundly a slave than she could imagine possible.

The following morning after breakfast Anne-Marie told O and Yvonne to come with her into her room. From her secretary she took a green leather coffer which she set on the bed and opened. The two girls were seated at her feet. 'Yvonne has told you nothing?' Anne-Marie asked of O. O shook her head. What was there for Yvonne to tell her? 'Nor Sir Stephen, of course. Well, here are the rings he wishes you to wear.' They were rings of dull stainless steel, like the iron in the iron-and-gold ring.

The metal was round, about the thickness of a pencil, the shape of each ring oblong: similar to the links of heavy chains. Anne-Marie showed O that each was composed of two U-shaped halves, one of which tenoned into the other. 'This is simply the trial model,' said she. 'It can be removed. Whereas, if you'll look closely, you'll see that here, in the permanent variety, there are spring catches inside the hollow prongs: one inserts the other half and it locks. Once locked, it can't be opened – can't be taken off. One would have to file the ring in two.' Each ring was as long as two little fingers, and just wide enough to admit one's little finger. From each ring was suspended, like a second link, or like the loop which supports the pendant of an ear-ring, a disk of the same metal and as large in its diameter as the ring was long. On one side, gold inlay; on the other, nothing. 'On the blank side,' said Anne-Marie, 'your name will be engraved, also your title, Sir Stephen's first and last names, and beneath that, a device: a crossed whip and riding-crop. Yvonne wears a similar disk on her collar. But you'll wear yours on your belly.' 'But –' O began. 'I know,' Anne-Marie interrupted, 'that's why I brought Yvonne in. Show your belly, Yvonne.' The red-haired girl rose and lay down on the bed. Anne-Marie opened her thighs and had O notice that one of her labia, midway down and close to its base, had been pierced: a clean hole, such as a ticket-puncher makes. A clean hole: the trial model ring would just pass through it. 'I'll make the hole for you in a moment or two, O,' said Anne-Marie, 'there's nothing to it, what takes time is putting the clamp in place: the epidermis outside and the membrane inside have to be sutured properly, the holes must coincide. It's much less painful than the whip.' 'But aren't you going to give me an anesthetic?' O cried, trembling. 'Certainly not,' replied Anne-Marie, 'you'll simply be tied, somewhat tighter than yesterday. That's altogether sufficient. Come.'

A week later, Anne-Marie removed the clamps and slipped the trial model in place. Light as it was – it was lighter than it looked, for it was hollow – it hung heavily. The hard metal, very visibly penetrating the flesh, resembled an instrument of torture; what would it be when the second ring was added and it hung even more heavily? This barbarous apparatus would immediately catch any glance. 'Of course,' Anne-Marie admitted when O made the remark, 'but you did understand what Sir Stephen wants, didn't you? You do now: whoever, at Roissy or elsewhere, Sir Stephen or anyone else, you too before the mirror, whoever lifts up your skirt will immediately see the rings on your belly, and, if he turns you around, the insignia on your buttocks. It's possible that you someday succeed in having the rings filed off, but you'll never get rid of the insignia.' 'I used to think,' said Colette, 'that tattoos could be removed very easily.' (It was she who, upon Yvonne's fair skin, just above the triangle of her belly, had tattooed the initials of Yvonne's master; the ornate blue script letters resembled embroidery.) 'O won't be tattooed.' Anne-Marie declared. O stared at Anne-Marie. Colette and Yvonne, dumbfounded, fell silent. Anne-Marie hesitated a moment. 'Well?' said O. 'Say

126

it.' 'Ah, my dear,' said Anne-Marie, 'I hardly dare. You will be marked with an iron. Sir Stephen sent me the iron two days ago.' 'Iron?' cried Yvonne. 'A red-hot one.'

From the first day, O had shared the life led in that house, a life of absolute and mandatory idleness relieved by monotonous distractions. The girls were free to take walks in the garden, to read, to draw, to play cards, to play patience. They could sleep in their bedrooms or stretch out in the sun for sunbaths. Sometimes they talked together, all of them, or talked in pairs, for hours on end, sometimes they remained sitting down for hours on end, at Anne-Marie's feet and in silence. The meal-hours were fixed, never changed, dinner at mid-day, candles on the table, tea was taken in the garden, and there was something absurd about the perfectly natural and matter-of-fact manner in which the two housemaids catered to these naked girls grouped around a ceremoniously laid table. In the evening, Anne-Marie designated one of them as her bed-companion for the night, sometimes the same girl slept with her several nights in a row. She caressed her and had herself caressed by her, usually towards dawn, would then go back to sleep again after having sent her back to her room. The violet curtains, never more than partially drawn, would lend a mauve tint of dawning day, and Yvonne said that Anne-Marie was as beautiful and loftily superb in her pleasure as she was indefatigable in her demands. None of them had ever seen her entirely naked. She opened or pulled up her white nylon night-gown, but never took it off. Neither the pleasure she may have tasted during the night nor her previous evening's choice of companion ever had any influence upon the following afternoon's decision which was invariably arrived at by drawing lots. At three o'clock, under the purple beech where the garden chairs were grouped round a circular white stone table, Anne-Marie would call for the box and the disks. Each girl would take a disk. She who drew the lowest number was therewith conducted into the music room and arranged upon the stage in the way O had been. Then – but not O, who was exempt until her departure – then she had simply to guess in which hand, right or left, Anne-Marie was holding a marble. The

127

wrong guess meant a flogging, the right one no flogging. Anne-Marie played the game with unimpeachable honesty, and if luck would so have it that a given girl was to be spared, she would be spared; or if flogged several days in succession, flogged she was. The torture of little Yvonne, who sobbed and cried out for her lover, was thus repeated four days running. Her spread thighs, like her chest striated with green veins, revealed pink flesh transpierced by the thick iron ring, finally set in place, and all the more striking in that Yvonne's pubic hair had been entirely shaven off. 'But why' O asked, 'and why the ring since you already have a disk on your collar?' 'He says that I am more naked when I'm shaved. I think the ring is to fasten me by.' Yvonne's green eyes, her little triangular face made O think of Jacqueline everytime she looked at her. And if Jacqueline were to go to Roissy? Some day or another, Jacqueline would pass this way, would be here, lying flat on this platform. 'I don't want to,' said O, 'I don't want to, I'll do nothing whatsoever to get her into this, I've already told her too much as it is.' But how well blows and irons suited Yvonne, how admirably well, how sweet were her moans, the sweat running down her limbs. For Anne-Marie had twice (but, up until now, only for Yvonne), handed her the whip and instructed her to strike. The first time, during the first minute, she'd wavered, at Yvonne's first scream recoiled, but when once she'd begun again and Yvonne had screamed anew, louder than before, she had been gripped by a terrible pleasure, a pleasure so piercing that she felt herself laughing with joy despite herself, and had had to overcome powerful impulses in order to decelerate the cadence of the blows she was delivering and not to strike with all the strength at her command. After that, she had remained at Yvonne's side the whole time Yvonne had remained bound, periodically kissing her. She probably resembled Yvonne in some manner. At least, Anne-Marie's similar feelings for them both indicated it. Was it O's silence, her docility that appealed to the woman? No sooner were O's cuts healed and scarring than: 'Oh, how I regret,' Anne-Marie said, 'not being able to have you whipped. When you come back . . . Well,

128

anyhow, I'm going to open you every day.' And every day when the girl in the music room was detached, O took her place until the hour when the bell rang for dinner. And Anne-Marie was right: it was perfectly true that, during those two hours, she could think of nothing save that she was open and of the ring hanging so heavily from her belly once the ring was placed there, that ring which weighed yet more heavily when the second link was added to it. Of nothing save her slavery and of the tokens of her slavery. One evening, coming in from the garden, Claire, accompanied by Colette, had approached O and examined her rings. They were still lacking an inscription. 'When did you enter Roissy?' asked Claire. 'Was it Anne-Marie who sent you there?'

'No,' said O. 'Anne-Marie sent me, it was two years ago. I'm going back the day after tomorrow.' 'But don't you belong to someone?' asked O. 'Claire belongs to me,' said Anne-Marie. 'Your master arrives tomorrow morning, O. You will sleep with me tonight.' The brief summer's night waned slowly, towards four in the morning the daylight drowned out the last of the stars. O, sleeping with her knees pressed together, was awakened by Anne-Marie's hand foraging between her thighs. But Anne-Marie wished only to wake her, wished only to have O caress her. Her eyes glistened in the early dawn light, and her grey hair, shot through with threads of black, cut short and pushed up by the pillow, nearer straight than waving, gave her the look of the mighty seigneur in exile, of the dauntless libertine. With her lips, O brushed the hard tips of her breasts, with her hand fondled the crack in her belly. Anne-Marie was swift to react, prompt to surrender – but it wasn't to O. The pleasure upon which she opened wide her eyes in the smiting glare of daylight was an anonymous pleasure, an impersonal one whereof O was the mere instrument. It mattered not at all to her whether O admired her smoothed and rejuvenated face, her fine panting mouth, of no matter to her whether O heard her moan when she nipped her teeth shut upon the crest of flesh hidden in the furrow of her belly. She simply seized O by the hair and pressed her face harder against her loins, and only

loosened her grip in order to tell her: 'Do it again.' O had
loved Jacqueline in a like manner. She had possessed Jacqueline, at least she'd thought so.

But the similarity of gestures signified nothing. O did not
possess Anne-Marie. No one possessed Anne-Marie. Anne-
Marie demanded, extracted caresses without concerning herself for what those who caressed her felt, and surrendered
herself with an insolent liberty. Still in all, she was tender and
gentle with O, kissed her mouth, kissed the tips of her breasts,
and hugged her yet an hour before sending her away. She had
removed O's irons. 'These hours,' she had said, 'are the last
when you'll sleep without wearing irons. Those that will be
put on you very shortly won't come off.' She had passed her
hand slowly and tenderly over O's buttocks, then had led her
into her dressing-room, the only one the house equipped with a
three-sided mirror, which was always kept closed. But now she
had opened it so that O could see herself. 'This is the last time
you'll see yourself intact,' she said. 'It's here, where you are so
round and smooth: Sir Stephen's initials will be burnt into you
here, on either side of the cleft dividing your buttocks. I'll
bring you back again to look at the mirror on the eve of your
departure. You'll not recognize yourself. But Sir Stephen is
right. Go sleep, O.' But her anguish kept O awake, and when
Monique came for her at ten o'clock, she had to help O bathe,
do her hair and paint her lips. O was shaking in every limb;
she had heard the gate open: Sir Stephen was there. 'Come
along, O,' said Yvonne, 'he's waiting for you.'

The sun was already high in the heavens, not a breath of air
stirred in the leaves of the beech: motionless, it seemed to have
turned into copper. Overwhelmed by the heat, the collie lay
at the foot of the tree, and as the sun had not yet wheeled behind the mass of the tree's foliage, rays shot through the outer
edges of the one branch which at that hour cast a shadow upon
the table: the table's stone top was spattered with bright warm
patches. Sir Stephen was standing, motionless also, beside the
table, Anne-Marie was sitting beside him. 'Here we are,' said
Anne-Marie when Yvonne had led O before her, 'the rings can
be set in place whenever you like, she has been pierced.' With-

out replying, Sir Stephen drew O into his arms, kissed her mouth and, raising her completely off the ground, lay her down on the table and bent over her where she lay. Then he kissed her again, caressed her eyebrows and her hair and, straightening up, said to Anne-Marie: 'Right away, if you don't mind.' Anne-Marie took the leather coffer she had brought with her from the house and set on a chair, and handed Sir Stephen the separated parts of the rings which bore O's name and his. 'Go ahead,' said Sir Stephen. Yvonne flexed O's knees and O felt the chill of the metal Anne-Marie was slipping through her perforated flesh. Just before snapping the second part of the link into the first, Anne-Marie carefully checked to make sure that the inlaid side was next to the thigh and the side carrying the inscription facing out. But the spring was so stiff that the two prongs wouldn't pass the catch. Yvonne had to be sent to fetch a hammer. O was made to sit up and, spreading her legs, they perched her on the edge of the slab of stone: using it as an anvil, upon it they butted first one and then the other of the female halves of the links, driving home the first and then the second of the male halves. Sir Stephen observed; Sir Stephen was silent. When it was done, he thanked Anne-Marie and helped O down off the table and onto her feet. She immediately perceived that these new irons were much heavier than the ones she had been wearing provisionally for the past several days. But these were the definitive ones. 'And now your mark – correct?' Anne-Marie asked Sir Stephen. Sir Stephen nodded his acquiescence, and supported the swaying O: he held her by the waist; she did not have her black corset on, but Sir Stephen's grip was so firm, and her waist so slim, that she seemed ready to break in two. Her haunches seemed rounder, her breasts looked heavier. In the music room, to which, following Anne-Marie and Yvonne, Sir Stephen more carried than guided O, Colette and Claire were sitting just in front of the stage. They rose as the others entered. On the stage was a large single-burner gas stove. Anne-Marie took straps from a cupboard and passing them round O's waist and ankles, bound her tightly to one of the columns. Her hands and feet were also bound. Drowning in terror, O felt Anne-Marie's hand upon

131

her buttocks, indicating the place where the iron was to be placed. She heard the hiss of a flame. In the perfect stillness, she heard a window being closed. She could have turned her head about and watched. She didn't have the strength to. One single abominable pain shrieked through her and as though lightningstruck stiffened her and sent her screaming against her bonds, and she never knew who it was had driven those two red-hot irons simultaneously into the flesh of her two buttocks, nor whose voice it had been that slowly counted to five, nor upon whose gesture the irons had been raised away. When she was unfastened, she collapsed into Anne-Marie's arms and had enough time, before darkness closed in upon her and before all her senses deserted her, to detect, between two great billows of night-time blackness, the livid visage of Sir Stephen.

Sir Stephen took O back to Paris ten days before the end of July. The irons threaded through the left lip of her sex and bearing the graven attestation that she was Sir Stephen's property dangled a third of the way down her thigh and with every step she took stirred between her legs like the clapper of a bell, the inscribed disk being heavier and hanging lower than the ring to which it was affixed. The marks imprinted by the branding-iron were three inches high and a half that in width, were dug into her flesh as though by a gouge, were about half an inch deep. The lightest touch applied to her bottom betrayed their presence to the finger. From these irons, from these marks O derived an insane pride. Had Jacqueline been there, instead of trying to hide the fact she bore them, as she had tried to conceal the traces left by Sir Stephen's riding-crop just before her departure, she would have run to find Jacqueline in order to exhibit them. But Jacqueline wasn't there and wouldn't be back for a week. René wasn't there either. During that week, O, upon Sir Stephen's request, had some day-dresses and some very light evening-dresses made; he dictated the patterns for each, these she could vary but not essentially depart from: a costume opening all the way down the front by means of a zipper (she already had similar dresses), the other model consisting in a full skirt which could be raised by a single movement, a corselet which came up to the breasts and a bolero which fastened about the neck. The bolero removed, the shoulders and breasts were left bare; and if one simply desired to see the breast, the bolero could be opened without taking it off. There was no question of a swimming suit: O couldn't wear one: the irons would have hung below it. Sir Stephen told her that it was summer-time, that she would swim in the nude when she swam. No question either of play suits or beach trousers. However, Anne-Marie, who had contrived these patterns, knowing the way in which Sir Stephen preferred to use O, had suggested a pair of trousers fitted with two long zippers, one on either side but, though unzipped, remaining up in front, thus, it would be possible to lower a rear flap without taking the garment off. But Sir Stephen rejected the proposal. It was true that he just about invariably used O as if she were a boy, when he didn't employ her mouth. But O had noticed that when she was near him he liked, at whatever moment, even when he did not desire her and as it were unthinkingly, mechanically, to take hold of her sex, seize and tug at her fleece, open her and rummage his hand inside her. O's own pleasure in grasping a similarly wet and burning Jacqueline in her contracting fingers was a constant reminder of the pleasure Sir Stephen took in doing the same thing to her. She appreciated why he would not wish to have to cope with unnecessary difficulties in order to obtain it.

Dressed in the twilled stripe or polka-dot, grey and white, navy blue and white, which O had selected for a pleated sunskirt and a trim-fitting, closed little bolero, or in more severe black nylon dresses, wearing hardly any make-up, hatless, her hair free, she had the look of a well brought-up little girl. Everywhere Sir Stephen took her she was thought to be his daughter, or his niece, the more so because he now used *tu* in addressing her and she went on saying *vous* to him. All alone together in Paris, walking along the streets, peering into shopwindows, strolling along the river banks where the cobblestones were dusty during that dry summer, they calmly came and went while passers-by smiled at them as happy people are treated to smiles. Sir Stephen would now and again push her

133

into an arched doorway, or into some impasse, into some dark place whence emerged gusts of cold cellar-air, and he would kiss her and tell her that he loved her. Stepping over the high sills of those little doors that are usually cut in the great gateway doors, O would catch her heels. At the further end of a courtyard clothes were out drying on a line or hanging from windows; her elbows leaning on the railing of a balcony, a blonde girl would gaze fixedly at them; a cat would skid with a swish between their legs. Thus they went strolling to the Gobelins, down the rue Saint-Marcel, up the rue Mouffetard, to the Temple, to the Bastille. Sir Stephen once steered O into a miserable hotel where the man in charge wanted at first to have them fill out the forms, but then said that he guessed it wasn't worth the trouble since they were only going to stay for an hour. In the room the wall-paper was blue with enormous gilded peonies, the window gave out upon an air shaft up which rose the smell of garbage-cans. Weak as the one bulb over the bed was, one could see rice-powder and hairpins scattered over the marble mantelpiece of the little fireplace. On the ceiling above the bed there was a great mirror.

Once, just once, Sir Stephen invited O to join him and two visiting countrymen for lunch. He came to get her an hour before she had been told to be ready. Instead of having her come to his place, he came to get her at the quai de Béthune, arriving a full hour before the time he had told her to be ready. O had bathed, but had still to do her hair, to put on her make-up, to get dressed. To her surprise, she saw Sir Stephen carrying a golf-club bag in his hand. But her surprise vanished when, Sir Stephen having told her to open the bag, she found that it contained an assortment of riding-crops, two of red leather and rather thick, two which were very slender and long and in black leather, plus a scourge furnished with very long green leather lashes each of which was looped in a bight at its end, then a dog-whip made of a single thick leather thong and whose handle was of braided leather, and finally some leather wristbands such as those at Roissy, and some rope. O arranged them neatly, side by side, on the unmade bed. Whatever the degree to which she was accustomed to these things, whatever her firmness, she was trembling; Sir Stephen took her in his arms. 'Which do you prefer, O?' But she could hardly speak and already felt the sweat running down from her armpits. 'Which do you prefer?' he repeated. 'You don't have any particular preference? Well anyhow,' he said in the face of her silence, 'you can help me first. Have you any nails?' having arranged the whips and crops in a decorative manner, he showed O that a panel of wainscotting between her mirror and the fireplace opposite her bed would be the ideal place to put them up. He hammered in the nails. Fitted into the ends of the handles of the whips and crops were rings by which they could be suspended from L-shaped nails; with L-shaped nails – and he had bent the nails in the shape of an L – one could take each whip or crop down and put it back, easily and without disturbing the others; and now, with the wristbands and the ropes, O would have, facing her bed, the complete panoply of the instruments used for her torture. It was a pretty display, as harmonious as the wheel and the pincers in the pictures of Saint Catherine's martyrdom, as the hammer and the nails, the crown of thorns and the lance and the scourges in the representations of the Passion. When Jacqueline came back . . . but this was also, precisely, for her benefit. She had to answer Sir Stephen's question: she couldn't, and he made his own choice: of the dog-whip.

In a tiny private dining room on the second floor of La Pérouse where figures out of Watteau in light, faintly faded colors on the dark walls resembled actors in a puppet theatre, O was installed on the divan bench, one of Sir Stephen's friends to her left in a chair, another to her right in another chair, and Sir Stephen, also in a chair, opposite her. She had already seen one of these men at Roissy, but she did not remember ever having been taken by him. The other was a tall young man with red hair and grey eyes; he was certainly no older than twenty-five. In three words Sir Stephen explained to them why he had invited O and what she was. Listening to him speak, O was once again astonished at the coarseness of his language. But, then again, how else could she expect to be qualified if not as a whore, a girl who said yes, consented, in the presence of three men not to mention the restaurant waiters who were still coming in and out, the meal still being in progress, to open her jacket and show her breasts whose points were very conspicuously painted and which, as one could very plainly see by the two purple furrows running across the white skin, had been recently beaten. The meal went on and on, and the two Englishmen drank a great deal. At coffee, when liqueurs had been brought, Sir Stephen pushed the table towards the other wall, and after having raised her skirt to show his friends how O had been marked and ironed, left her to them. The man she had met at Roissy wasted no time and was finished in a hurry: without rising from his chair, without touching her, he bade her kneel in front of him, take his sex and caress it, then he ejaculated into her mouth; that accomplished, he ordered her to adjust his clothing, and, bidding everyone good day, left. But the red-haired boy, overwhelmed by O's submissiveness, by the sight of her irons and the lacerations he had seen on her body, instead of springing upon her, as O expected, took her by the hand and, completely ignoring the waiter's knowing smiles, went down the stairs, hailed a taxi, and took her to his hotel room. He did not let her go till nightfall, after having frenziedly belaboured her belly and behind, whence he drew blood, for he was thick and furiously stiff and completely out of his head to find himself all of a sudden and for the first time free to penetrate a woman wherever he chose and to have a woman embrace him as he had shortly before seen that it was possible to make a woman embrace one (and as, hitherto, he had never dared ask any woman to do). When O arrived at Sir Stephen's the next day towards two o'clock in answer to his summons, she found his face grave, careworn, he looked older. 'Eric has fallen madly in love with you, O,' he said to her. 'He came here this morning and begged me to give you back your freedom, he said he wants to marry you. He wants to save you. You know what I do to you, O, you know what I am going to keep on doing to you as long as you're mine, and if you're mine you're not free to refuse; but, you also know that you are always free to refuse to be mine. I told him that. He's coming back at three.' O began to laugh. 'Why,' she said, 'don't you think it's a bit late in the day for that? You're crazy, the pair of you. If Eric hadn't come to see you this morning, what would you have done with me this afternoon? We'd have gone for a walk and nothing else? Just for a walk? Then let's take a little walk; or why did you telephone to me? Or perhaps you didn't mean to? If so, I'll be going –'

'No,' said Sir Stephen. 'I'd have telephoned you anyhow, O, but not to take you out for a walk. I wished to –'

'Say it.'

'Come with me, that will be simpler.'

He rose and opened a door in the wall across from the fire-place. It was a door similar to the one which led into his office downstairs, and O had always thought it the door to what had once been a closet and was now sealed. She saw a very small boudoir, freshly painted, hung with dark red silk; half of the room was occupied by a curved stage flanked by two columns, identical to the platform in the music room at Samois. 'The walls and ceiling are sound-proofed, aren't they,' said O, 'and the door is padded, isn't it, and you've had a double window put in?' Sir Stephen nodded. 'But since when?' 'It's been done since your return.' 'And why?' 'Why what?' 'Why have I waited until now?' 'Because I have been waiting to put you into other men's hands. Now I am going to punish you. I have never punished you, O.'

'But I am yours,' said O, 'punish me if you like. And when Eric comes –'

And when an hour later, brought into the presence of an O spread grotesquely open between the two columns, the young man turned white, stammered and vanished. O expected never to see him again. But she encountered him at Roissy towards the end of Stepember, and he took charge of her for three days in a row and mistreated her savagely.

IV

THE OWL

If O hesitated to speak to Jacqueline of what René very justly termed her true condition, it was because she no longer understood it. Anne-Marie had indeed told her that, by the time she left Samois, she would undergo a change. She had never believed that the change would be so drastic. Jacqueline home again, and more radiant and fresh than ever, O felt no greater need to hide herself when she bathed or dressed than when she had been alone. Jacqueline, however, took so little interest in anything apart from herself that it had to be by accident that, two days after her return, she entered the bathroom at the very moment when O, stepping out of the tub, allowed the irons hanging from her belly to strike against the enamel: the sound attracted Jacqueline's attention. She turned her head and at the same time saw the zig-zagging welts streaking O's thighs and breasts and the disk suspended between her legs.

'What's all that?' she exclaimed.

'Sir Stephen,' O replied. Then she added in a matter-of-fact way: 'René gave me to him. He clipped a tag on me; look.' And all the while drying herself with the bath-towel, she walked over to Jacqueline who, thunderstruck, had sat down on the lacquered bathroom stool; O came close, close enough to enable Jacqueline to take the disk between her fingers and read what was written on it; then, lifting the towel away and turning about, she pointed to the S and the H wrought in her buttocks, and said: 'He also had me stamped with his initials. The others are whip marks. He generally whips me himself, but he also has me whipped by his negro servant, the woman he has for a housekeeper.' Jacqueline stared at O, unable to utter a

138

word. O began to laugh, then tried to kiss Jacqueline; Jacqueline, horrified, thrust her away and fled into the bedroom. O finished drying herself and then, perfectly tranquil, put on her perfume, brushed her hair. She put on her corset, her stockings, her slippers, and when she closed the door behind her met Jacqueline's glance in the mirror: Jacqueline was seated before O's dressing-table and combing her hair without seeming to know what she was doing. 'Would you tighten my corset, please,' O said. 'How surprised you are – should you be? René's in love with you – has he told you so? No?' 'I don't understand anything,' Jacqueline said; and, straightway revealing what amazed her most of all: 'you look as if you were proud of it. I don't understand.'

'When René takes you to Roissy, you'll understand. Have you started to sleep with him yet?'

Blood rose in a rush to Jacqueline's face; she shook her head; so transparently false was the denial that O burst out laughing again.

'Little liar. Come, Jacqueline, my love, don't be silly. Why not sleep with him? You have every right to. And that's no reason for turning up your nose at me. Come, let me caress you, I want to tell you a story. It's all about Roissy.'

Had Jacqueline dreaded a violent display of jealousy on O's part, or was it from relief that she yielded, or simply because she loved the patience, the slowness, the passion with which O caressed her? She yielded. 'Tell me the story,' she said afterwards. 'I will,' said O, 'but first kiss the points of my breasts. It's high time you got accustomed to that if you want to be in any way useful to René.' Jacqueline obeyed, obeyed so well that she brought moans of pleasure from O. 'Tell me,' she repeated.

Accurate and clear as it may have been, and despite the material proof she herself constituted of the truth of what she related, O's story struck Jacqueline as the ravings of a madman.

'You mean to say you're going back there in September?'

'After we return from the Midi,' said O. 'I'll take you there, or René will.'

'For a look, fine, but only for a look,' said Jacqueline.

'Of course. You can go for a look,' said O, who was convinced, however, that if one went it would be for more than a look; and, she said to herself, that if she could simply induce Jacqueline past the gates of Roissy, Sir Stephen would be altogether satisfied with her – and that, Jacqueline once inside, there would be valets enough and chains and whips a-plenty, more than was needed to teach Jacqueline obedience. She already knew that in the villa Sir Stephen had rented near Cannes, where she was to spend August with René, Jacqueline and himself and Jacqueline's younger sister, whom Jacqueline had asked permission to bring along – not that she enormously wanted to, but because her mother had been after her night and day until she had obtained O's consent – she knew that the room she was to occupy and in which Jacqueline would hardly be able to refuse taking at least afternoon naps with her, when René wouldn't be there, was separated from Sir Stephen's room by a partition which looked blind but which, behind false lattice-work and trellis decorations, was transparent: by raising a shade on his side, Sir Stephen would be as well able to see and overhear everything that went on in the room as if he were standing by the bedside. Jacqueline, caressed and kissed by O, would be within full view of Sir Stephen, and when she found out, it would be too late. O tasted a sweet pleasure in thinking of how she would betray Jacqueline, for she had felt it an insult, the scornful manner in which Jacqueline had eyed this condition of a branded and flogged slave, this condition whereof O was proud.

O had never been in the Midi before. The steady blue sky, the scarcely stirring sea, the motionless pines under the high sun, it all looked mineral and hostile to her. 'No real trees,' she thought with a sad sigh as she gazed at these aromatic shrubberies, dry and brittle, beneath which the stones, and even the lichens, were warm to the touch. 'The sea doesn't smell like the sea,' she said to herself. She blamed the sea for heaving up nothing better than ugly little scraps of yellowish seaweed which resembled animal droppings, reproached the

140

sea for being too blue, for always lapping at the shore in the same place. But in the garden of the villa, which was an old renovated farmhouse, one was far away from the sea. On both sides, high walls screened one from the neighbours; the wing where the domestics were lodged gave upon the court by which one entered, on the other side of the house; on this side, the garden side, was O's room, opening straight onto a second-floor terrace and looking east. The tops of tall black laurels soared past the over-lapped hollow tiles which served as a parapet to the terrace; a lattice of roses protected it from the mid-day sun, the red tiling that composed its floor was the same as in her bedroom. Save for the partition separating O's room from Sir Stephen's, all the walls were whitewashed. The thick rugs strewn over the tiles were in white cotton, the curtains in heavy white-and-yellow striped linen. There were two arm-chairs, each upholstered in the same material, and blue Cambodian floor-cushions. By way of further furniture, there was a very fine Regency bureau in chestnut, and a very long and very narrow provincial table, limed oak and polished like a mirror. O hung up her dresses in a wardrobe. She used the bureau as a dressing-table. Little Nathalie had been installed in a room near O's, and in the morning, when she knew O was taking her sunbath out on the terrace, she would come out and lie down beside her.

She was a pale-skinned girl, not tall, chubby but neverthe-less delicately-featured, with eyes slanting towards her tem-ples like those of her sister, but dark and shining, with the result she looked oriental. Her black hair was cut short in thick bangs coming down to just above her eyebrows and, in back, fell straight to her nape. She had firm, tremulous little breasts, and a child's undeveloped hips. She too had come upon O by surprise, dashing out upon the terrace where she expected to find her sister and where, instead she found O alone and lying on her stomach upon a floor-cushion. But what had revolted Jacqueline had left Nathalie wonderstruck, smitten with de-sire and curiosity; she had questioned her sister. Jacqueline, relating to her just what she had learned from O herself, sup-posed that Nathalie would be horrified, as she herself had been;

but far from it, it in no way altered Nathalie's emotions. She had fallen in love with O. She managed to keep still for more than a week, then one Sunday afternoon she successfully arranged to be alone with O.

The weather was less warm that day than it had been hitherto. René, who had spent part of the morning swimming, was napping on the couch in a cool ground-floor room. Annoyed to see that he preferred to sleep, Jacqueline had joined O in her alcove. The sea and the sun had rendered her blonder than ever: her hair, her eyebrows, her lashes, the fur between her thighs and under her arms seemed powdered with silver, and as she was wearing no make-up at all, her mouth was the same pink as the pink flesh of her open sex. In order that Sir Stephen – whose presence, O said to herself, she would surely have divined, noticed, somehow sensed, had she been in Jacqueline's place – could see every bit of her, O took care to flex Jacqueline's knees and to maintain her legs wide apart for a while and in the full light of the lamp she had turned on at the bedside. The shutters were drawn, the room was almost dark despite the slivers of light that penetrated between cracks in the wood. For nigh on to an hour Jacqueline moaned under O's caresses, and finally, her nipples erected, her arms flung over her head, clutching the wooden bars at the head of her bed, she began to scream when O, dividing the lips fringed with pale hair, set quietly and slowly to biting the tiny inflamed morsel of flesh protruding from the cowl formed by the juncture of those sweet and delicate little labia. O felt it heat and rise under her tongue, and, nipping mercilessly, fetched cry after cry from Jacqueline until she broke like a pane of glass, and relaxed, soaked from joy. Then O sent her into her room, where she went to sleep; she was awake again and ready when at five René came to take her and Nathalie down to the water for a sail; they used to go sailing in the late afternoon, when a bit of breeze usually rose. 'Where is Nathalie?' René asked.

Nathalie wasn't in her bedroom, she wasn't anywhere in the house. They went to look for her in the garden, she wasn't there either. René hunted as far as the little grove of cork-oaks which prolonged the garden; no answer to his calls. 'She may have gone down to the cove,' he suggested, 'maybe she's already in the boat.' They set off without looking further for her. It was then that O, lying on her cushion on the terrace, through the balustrade of tiles caught a glimpse of Nathalie running towards the house. She got up, slipped on her bathrobe – she was naked, it was still warm at that hour – and was tying the belt when Nathalie, arriving like a fury, hurled herself upon her. 'She's gone,' she gasped, 'she's gone at last. I heard you, O, I heard everything, I was listening at the door. You kiss her, don't you O? You hug her and you caress her, don't you? Why don't you hug me too? Why don't you caress me too? Why? Because I have black hair and because I'm not pretty? She doesn't love you, O, she doesn't, but I do.' And she burst into tears and sobbed. 'Nathalie,' O said, 'be still, Nathalie.'

She pushed the little girl into a deckchair, told her to stay there, took a big handkerchief from her bureau (it was one of Sir Stephen's handkerchiefs), and when Nathalie's sobbing had subsided somewhat, wiped away her tears. Nathalie asked to be forgiven, begged to be, kissed O's hands.

'Even if you don't want to hug me and kiss me, O, keep me here with you, won't you? Keep me with you all the time. If you had a dog, you'd take care of him, wouldn't you? If you don't want to kiss me but if you want to beat me, you can, but don't send me away, let me stay here.'

'Be still, Nathalie, you don't have any idea what you're talking about, so hush,' said O, speaking in a whisper.

Also speaking in a whisper, and slipping down to clutch O's knees, the little one replied: 'Oh yes I do.'

'Do you?'

'I saw you on the terrace yesterday morning. I saw the initials on you, and I saw all those black and blue marks. And Jacqueline told me –'

'Told you what?'

'Where you were, O, and what they did to you.'

'She talked to you about Roissy?'

'She told me you've been – that you were –'

'That I was what?'

'That you have iron rings on.'

'Yes,' said O, 'and what else?'

'And that Sir Stephen beats you every day.'

'Yes,' O said again, 'and he's going to come here in a few moments. Go along, Nathalie.'

Nathalie didn't move; she raised her head towards O, and O met her gaze. It was one of total adulation.

'Teach me, O, please, please teach me,' she said, 'I want to be like you. I'll do everything you tell me to do. Promise to take me with you when you go back there where Jacqueline said you were going to go.'

'You're a little girl,' said O, 'you're too little.'

'No I'm not, O, I'm fifteen, I'm not too little,' she cried, furious, 'I'm not too little just ask Sir Stephen if I am, just ask Sir Stephen,' she repeated – for Sir Stephen had just then entered.

Nathalie was allowed to stay near O, and was given the promise that she would be taken to Roissy. But Sir Stephen forbade O to teach her the least caress, to kiss her even upon the mouth, or to let Nathalie kiss her; he intended to have her reach Roissy without having been touched by any hands or lips whatsoever. Conversely, since she didn't want to be separated from O, he required that she see O caressing not only Jacqueline but caressing and giving herself to him, and that Nathalie be whipped by himself or Norah, as O was. The kisses with which O covered her sister, O's mouth upon Jacqueline's mouth made Nathalie tremble with jealousy and hatred. Cowering on the rug in the alcove at the foot of O's bed like little Dinarzade at the foot of Sheherazade's bed, she watched every time O was tied to the wooden bedstead, watched her writhe under the riding crop, watched the kneeling O humbly receive the thick, uprisen sex of Sir Stephen in her mouth, watched the prostrate O spread her own buttocks with her own hands to open the passage into her behind, watched all that with no other emotions save admiration, impatience, and envy.

O may perhaps have counted too heavily at once upon the indifference and the sensuality of Jacqueline, Jacqueline may have naively judged that by giving herself so liberally to O she was endangering her relationship with René; at any rate, Jacqueline suddenly ceased to be willing to make love with O. At about the same time it appeared that she was holding René (with whom she spent almost every night and every day), somewhat at arm's length. To be sure, with him she had never behaved like someone wildly in love. She considered him coolly, and when she smiled at him, the smile never reached her eyes. The while supposing that she was as abandoned with him as with her, which struck her as likely, O could not keep from thinking that, abandoned or not, Jacqueline was hardly committed by her sentiments; whereas one had the feeling that René was completely in the blind grip of the desire he had for her, was as if paralyzed by a love he had never hitherto experienced, an uneasy, troubled love, unsafe, unsure of being returned, and which dreads lest it offend. René lived, René slept in the same house that sheltered Sir Stephen, under the same roof as O, he breakfasted, lunched, went out with, strolled with Sir Stephen, with O, spoke to them: but he didn't see them, he didn't hear what they said to him. He saw, he heard through them, saw and heard something on the other side of them; and, in a silent, harassing effort, like the efforts one makes in dreams to jump onto a moving streetcar, to hang onto the railing of a collapsing bridge, sought to get at the underlying explanation of Jacqueline, the fundamental thing about Jacqueline, the truth concerning Jacqueline, which must exist somewhere within her golden hide, as behind the porcelain exterior there must inevitably be some little mechanism which makes the doll cry. 'Ah,' thought O, 'here it is, come at last, the day I've always been so afraid would come: when for René I'd turn into a shadow belonging to a past life, a life that has been led and that is now gone by. And I am not even sad, now that it has come, and I only feel sorry for him, pity is all I feel, and I can see him every day without feeling hurt that he no longer desires me, without bitterness, without regret. And yet, is it not odd that, only a few weeks ago, I ran halfway across Paris to beg him to tell me that he loved me. Was that my love for him? Was that all it was? So light a thing, so easily consoled? Consolation? But it does not even require that. I am happy. Had he then but to give me to Sir Stephen, was that enough to detach me from him? Has new love come so easily in another's arms?' But, objectively now, what was René next to Sir Stephen? Threads of paper, strings of straw – such in actual truth were the ties whereby he had bound her to him, and which he had so quickly severed; and that quick, that easy sunderance was what those so frail ties symbolized. Whereas what peaceful security, what reassurance, what delight, this iron ring which pierces flesh and weighs eternally, this mark that will remain forever, the master's hand which lays you down to rest on a couch of rock, the love of a master who is capable of pitilessly appropriating unto himself that which he loves. And, by way of final conclusion, O told herself that she had only loved René as a means for learning of love and for finding out how to give herself better, as a slave, as an ecstatic slave, to Sir Stephen. But thus to see René, who with her had been so free – and she had loved him for this freedom – walking as though in hobbles, as though his legs were caught in the waters and reeds of a lake whose surface looks still, but whose currents move swiftly further down and out of sight, this excited O's hatred against Jacqueline. Did René perceive that hatred, through imprudence did O allow him a glimpse of it? She committed an error. They had one afternoon gone to Cannes, together but alone, to a hairdresser, then they'd had some ice-cream on the terrace of the Réserve. Superb in a pair of black slacks and a black sweater, Jacqueline set even the sparkling gaiety of children in shadow, so smooth was she, so golden, so sleek and tough and so brightly fair in the broad blazing sun, so insolent, so impervious. She told O she had a rendezvous with the director she had worked with in Paris; she said it had to do with some outdoor shots, mountain scenes, they'd probably go up beyond Saint-Paul de Vence. Then the young man – the director – showed up, there he was, he was decent, clear-eyed, sure. He said nothing, there wasn't any need to. One had but to look at the way he looked at Jacqueline. He was in love with her, that didn't need saying. Anything strange about that? Nothing at all; but what was strange, however, was Jacqueline.

Half-reclining in one of those large adjustable beach-chairs, Jacqueline listened to him – he was talking now, of times and places, dates to set, arrangements to make, and the difficulty of getting one's hands on enough money to finish the film he'd got a fair start on. With Jacqueline he employed the familiar *tu*, she replied with nodded yesses and noes, her eyes half-closed. O was seated opposite Jacqueline, the young man between them. It was very easy to see that Jacqueline, from below lowered eyelids, was on the watch for signs of desire in the young man's face; it was the way she always watched, always supposing that no one noticed that she was watching. But the strangest thing of all was to see the uneasiness in her while she watched, the expectancy, the limp hands trailing beside her, the worry in that unsmiling, solemn face, the expression of anxious concern O had never seen her adopt in front of René. A fleeting smile lingered for a second near Jacqueline's lips when O bent forward to put her glass of cold water back on the table, and when their glances met: O understood that Jacqueline realized her game had been detected. Which didn't fluster Jacqueline one little bit; it was O who reddened. 'Too warm in the sun?' Jacqueline enquired. 'We'll take off in a couple of minutes. The sun's wonderful, though, isn't it? It feels fine.' Then she smiled again, but this time, raising her eyes towards her interlocutor, her smile was one of such tender abandon that one would have thought nothing in the world could have stopped him from catching her in his arms and kissing her. But no. He was too young to know that immodesty can also inhabit stillness and silence. He let Jacqueline stand up, shook hands with her, said good-bye to her. She'd phone him. He said good-bye again, this time to the shadow O constituted for him, and, standing on the sidewalk, watched their black Buick move off down the avenue, twixt the houses flaming under the sun and the excessively blue sea. The palm trees looked as if they'd been jig-sawed out of sheet-metal, the strollers like ill-cast wax statues animated by some extremely queer mechanism. 'You like him as much as all that?' O asked Jacqueline when the car had left the town and had climbed upon the upper cliff-road.

'That any concern of yours?' Jacqueline replied.

'It concerns René,' O returned.

'What also concerns René and Sir Stephen and if I've understood the situation at all well a hell of a lot of others too,' Jacqueline said, 'is that you aren't sitting right. You're going to wrinkle your dress.' O didn't stir. 'And, according to what I have been further given to understand,' Jacqueline went on, 'you aren't supposed to cross your legs either. Right?' But O was no longer listening to her. What did Jacqueline's threats mean to her? If Jacqueline were threatening to betray O for that exceedingly venial sin, did she fancy this a way to prevent O from betraying her to René? It wasn't that O didn't have the desire to. But René would not be able to bear learning that Jacqueline had lied to him, nor that she wanted to do as she liked independently of him. How was one to get Jacqueline to understand that, if she kept still, it was to avoid seeing René lose face, go pale and perhaps be so weak as not to punish Jacqueline? That it was, even more so, from fear of seeing René's rage turn upon her, O, the bearer of evil tidings, the betrayer. How was one to tell Jacqueline that she would say nothing, without at the same time having the look of making a deal with her, you play ball with me and I'll play ball with you? For Jacqueline was thinking that O was petrified with terror, with a terror that made her freeze at the thought of what would be inflicted upon her if Jacqueline were to talk.

By the time they got out of the car in the court of the old villa, they were no longer speaking to one another. Without glancing at O, Jacqueline plucked a white geranium from amongst those growing along the edge of the house. O was close enough behind her to smell the keen, strong odour of the leaves Jacqueline was crumbling between her fingers. Did she think thus to mask the odour of her own sweat, which was gluing the finely-woven sweater to her armpits and which was staining it darker there? In the red-tiled and whitewashed living room, René was alone. 'You're late,' he said when they walked in.

'Sir Stephen's waiting for you in the other room,' he added, speaking to O. 'He needs you. He isn't in a very good mood.'

Jacqueline exploded into laughter; O stared at her and flushed.

'You could have selected another occasion,' said René, misinterpreting Jacqueline's laugh and O's embarrassment.

'Oh, that's not what it's all about,' said Jacqueline, 'but, René, you've simply no idea, your faithful little servant isn't always . . . so damned obedient when you're not around. Take a look at her dress. Rumpled and mussed, I'd say.'

O was standing in the centre of the room, facing René. He told her to turn around. She couldn't, she was rooted to the spot.

'She also has a way of crossing her legs,' Jacqueline continued, 'but, of course, that doesn't show. Nor, in looking at her, that she has another little way of picking up boys.'

'That's not true!' O cried. 'You're the one who picks up boys,' and she sprang upon Jacqueline. René intercepted her hand as it was about to strike Jacqueline, and she was struggling in its grip for the pleasure of feeling less strong than he, of being at his mercy, when, lifting her head, she caught sight of Sir Stephen in the doorway. Sir Stephen was staring at her. Jacqueline had backed away towards the couch, her little face hardened from fear and anger, and O sensed that, busy as he was holding her still, all René's attentions were concentrated upon Jacqueline. She ceased fighting, relaxed and, stricken at the thought of being in the wrong under the very eyes of Sir Stephen, reiterated, this time in a low voice, that 'It's not true, I swear to you it isn't true.'

Without a word, and without a glance at Jacqueline, Sir Stephen gestured to René to release O, and to O to leave the room. He followed her; but, on the other side of the door, immediately thrust up against the wall, her sex and breasts seized by Sir Stephen, her mouth forced open by his tongue, O moaned from happiness and deliverance. The tips of her breasts stiffened beneath Sir Stephen's hand. He dug his other hand so roughly into her belly that she thought she might faint. Would she ever dare tell him that no pleasure, no joy, nothing she even imagined ever approached the happiness she felt before the freedom wherewith he made use of her, before

149

the idea that he knew there were no precaution, no limits he had to observe in the manner whereby he sought his pleasure in her body. Her certitude that when he touched her, whether it be to caress or beat her, that when he ordered her to do something it was uniquely because he wanted her to do it and for his sole pleasure, the certitude that he made allowances for nothing, was concerned for nothing but his own desire, so overwhelmed O that, every time she had proof of it, and often even when she simply thought about it, a fiery vestment, a red-hot corselet extending from shoulders to knees seemed to descend over her. As she was there, standing pinned against the wall, eyes shut, murmuring I love you, I love you when there was breath in her to murmur, Sir Stephen's nevertheless cool hands, cool as well-water in contact with the fire consuming her, the fire which traveled up and down within her, burned her still more. He quit her gently, smoothing the skirt down over her wet thighs, shutting the bolero over her quivering breasts. 'Come, O, I need you.' Then O, opening her eyes, suddenly saw that there was someone else there.

This large, naked, whitewashed room, in every respect similar to the living room, also opened by a wide French door out upon the garden, and upon the terrace between the house and the garden, sitting in a wicker chair, cigarette between his lips, a sort of shave-pated giant, his enormous belly stretching his shirt open and ready to burst his trousers, was staring at O. He rose and moved towards Sir Stephen, who was pushing O before him. O then saw, hanging from the end of a watch-chain, not a watch, but the Roissy emblem. However, Sir Stephen introduced him politely to O, presenting him as 'the Commander' without citing his last name; and for the first time since she'd had any contact with a member of the Roissy brotherhood (with the exception of Sir Stephen), she found, to her surprise, her hand being kissed. They all three returned to the room, leaving the door open; Sir Stephen went to the fireplace in the corner and rang. Upon the Chinese table next to the divan O saw a bottle of whisky, a siphon and glasses. It therefore hadn't been to have drinks brought that he'd rung. She also noticed a large cardboard carton sitting on the floor near the fireplace. The Roissy man had sat down in another wicker chair; Sir Stephen was half-seated on the round table, pensive, swaying one leg. O, who had been motioned towards the divan, had in sitting obediently raised her skirt: under her thighs she felt the soft cotton piqué of the Provençal covering. It was Norah who entered. Sir Stephen ordered her to undress O and to take her clothing away. O let the woman remove her bolero, her dress, the whaleboned belt that constricted her waist, her sandals. Directly she was naked, Norah left, and O, once again under the sway of Roissy robot-like obedience to the rule, certain that Sir Stephen desired nothing but absolute docility from her, remained standing in the middle of the room, her eyes bent downward and it was thus she rather guessed than saw Nathalie slip in through the open French door, like Jacqueline dressed in black, barefoot and mute. Sir Stephen had probably made some previous explanation regarding Nathalie; he at any rate now did no more than name her to his visitor, who posed no questions, and asked the girl to pour the drinks. As soon as they had been given their whisky, their soda-water and their ice (and in the silence, the tinkling of the ice-cubes against the glasses made a tremendous racket), the Commander, glass in hand, got up from his wicker chair, where he had remained seated while Norah had undressed O, and approached her. O thought that he was going to take her belly or breast in his free hand. But he did not touch her, he simply came up and took a long close look at her, at her parted lips, at her parted knees. He turned around her, inspecting her breasts, her thighs, her buttocks, and this silent inspection, this gigantic body so near to her, so intimidated, so confused O that she did not know whether she desired to flee or, quite to the contrary, whether she desired the Commander to crush her beneath his immense bulk. She was in such a state that she forgot herself altogether and raised her eyes towards Sir Stephen for help. He understood what the trouble was, smiled, came up to her and, taking her two hands, drew them behind her back and held them pinioned there in one of his. She slid back against him, her eyes shut, and it was in a dream – or at least, if not in dream, in the twilight of a half-slumbering weariness similar to that one when, as a child, only partially emerged from anesthesia, but still thought to be unconscious by the nurses, she'd heard them talking about her, about her hair, about her pallor, about her flat belly where the down had only begun to grow – that she now heard the un-known Commander compliment Sir Stephen upon her, parti-cularly stressing the pleasing effect created by somewhat heavy breasts in contrast with a narrow waist, and by somewhat more massive, longer, more visible irons than was customary. It seemed to her that Sir Stephen must have promised to lend her to the Commander the following week, since the Comman-der was thanking him for something, apparently for that. And now Sir Stephen, having been thanked, was pressing her neck between thumb and forefinger, whispering to her to wake up, and to go up to her room and wait, with Nathalie.

Had she cause to be so upset? and to be irritated by Nathalie who, as though drunk with delight at the thought of seeing O opened by someone else than Sir Stephen, was dan-cing a kind of wild Indian war-dance around her, exclaiming: 'Do you really think he'll go into your mouth too, O? You should have seen how he looked at your mouth. Oh, how lucky you are that people like you. I'll bet anything he'll whip you: he looked three times in a row at the marks where you've been whipped. At least, while he's whipping you you won't have to think about Jacqueline all the time.'

'But I don't think about Jacqueline all the time,' O replied. 'You're as silly as you can be.'

'Oh no I'm not silly,' said the little girl, 'I know that you miss her.'

It was true; but not completely. Or there was more to the truth than that. What O missed wasn't strictly speaking Jac-queline, but the use of a girl's body, a body with which she could do as she liked. Nathalie – there was nothing to prevent her from taking Nathalie, she could have, and the one reason she didn't was the knowledge that Nathalie would be given to her at Roissy, in a few weeks' time, and that it would be pri-marily before her and by her and thanks to her that Nathalie would be surrendered to the corporation. The barrier of air, of

space, of, in fine, nothing at all that separated her from Nathalie.
– she yearned to break down that barrier, and at the same
time she relished being forced to wait. She told this to Nathalie.
But Nathalie didn't believe it, 'Oh, no,' she insisted, 'it's not
me, if Jacqueline were here you'd caress her just like that.'
'Certainly,' said O, laughing. 'So there, you see,' said the child.
How was O to make her understand – and was there any point
in trying? – that, no, O was not so very much in love with
Jacqueline, nor for that matter with Nathalie, nor with any
girl in particular, but simply with girls because they were girls,
the way one can be in love with one's own image – always finding the others more arousing and lovelier than one finds one's
own self. The pleasure she tasted in seeing a girl pant under her
caresses, in seeing her eyes grow vague, swim, her eyelids close,
in stiffening the tips of a girl's breasts with one's lips and teeth,
in burrowing into her by thrusting one's hand into her belly or
a finger into her behind – in feeling her squeeze one's finger,
one's hand, in hearing her sigh, moan, cry – ah that! that she
adored: if that pleasure was intense, incisive, it was only because it made her think constantly of the pleasure she could
receive from the girl in her turn, when in her turn her muscles
contracted round the finger, round the hand holding her, when
she herself would sigh, would moan; yes, that she adored, except that she could not conceive of thus giving herself to a girl,
of giving herself the way a girl gave herself to her, but only to
a man. It also seemed to her, furthermore, that the girls she
caressed belonged by all rights to the man to whom she herself
belonged, and that she was there in a rôle, and that this rôle
was a procuress. Had Sir Stephen entered at some time in the
course of the past few days, had he come in while she had been
caressing Jacqueline during the siesta hour when Jacqueline
had made a habit of coming to her room, she would have exerted force, and without the faintest reluctance or remorse, why
no, with a total pleasure, have spread Jacqueline's legs with
both her hands, spread them wide for Sir Stephen if he'd have
desired to possess her instead of simply looking through the
place where the lattice-work concealed the gap in the partition-
wall, as he had done. She, O, she was fit for the hunt, she was

a naturally trained bird of prey that would rise and strike and bring home the quarry, every time. And indeed ... It was at this point, as with beating heart she thought again of Jacqueline's delicate and so very pink lips behind the blonde fur of her sex, of the still more delicate, still pinker ring hidden between her buttocks, the ring she'd dared force only three times, it was at this point she heard Sir Stephen stir in his room. She knew he could see her, even though she could not see him, and once again she felt that she was fortunate to be exposed thus, openly, constantly, fortunate in this prison wherein his constant gaze enclosed her. Little Nathalie had sat down on the white carpet in the middle of the room, poised like a fly in a saucer of milk, but O, standing up in front of the bow-legged bureau she used as a dressing-table, and above which she saw herself from head to waist in the antique mirror, a little greenish, or mossy, as though submarine, that image ... it made her think of those engravings dating from the later eighteenth century, engravings showing women wandering naked in the subdued light of their apartments, in the height of the summer's heat. When Sir Stephen pushed at the door, she spun around so swiftly that the irons between her thighs knocked against one of the brass drawer-pulls, and jingled.

'Nathalie,' said Sir Stephen, 'go get the white box downstairs in the room where we were all sitting.'

Nathalie returned with the carton. She put it upon the bed. She opened it and, one by one, took out and removed from their paper wrappings the objects it contained, and handed them one after another to Sir Stephen. They were masks. They were head-dresses and masks at the same time, they were intended to cover the entire head, everything except the eyes – there were two holes for the eyes – and the mouth and chin. All sorts of masks: sparrow-hawk, falcon, owl, fox, lion, bull, but only animal masks, scaled to human proportions, fully detailed made of real fur or feathers, the eye-socket surrounded by eyelashes if the creature in question (such as the lion), had eyelashes, and the pelt or plumage descending to below the wearer's shoulders, upon which the mask sat. A strap inside when tightened or loosened adjusted the mask so that it squared

154

up exactly with one's nostrils and upper lip and lay tight against one's cheeks. The shell was reinforced by an armature, which kept the entire thing's shape rigid. Before the other, the full-length mirror, O tried on each of the masks. The most curious of them all, and the one which simultaneously transformed her the most and seemed the most natural on her, was one of the owl-masks (there were two of them): its plumage in tans and browns blended with her bronzed skin; the hood of feathers almost entirely concealed her shoulders, descending, behind, to halfway down her back, and, in front, to where her breasts began. Sir Stephen had her remove the rouge from her lips; then, when she had removed the mask, said to her: 'You'll be an owl for the Commander. But O, I'm sorry to have to tell you that you'll be on a leash. Nathalie, in the upper drawer of my secretary you'll find a chain and a pair of pliers.'

Nathalie returned with the chain and the pliers. Sir Stephen pried open the last link on the chain and, slipping it through the second link O wore at her belly, bent it shut again. The chain, similar to the kind used for dogs – it was that kind – was some four or five feet long, and ended in a leather loop. Once again O donned her owl-mask; and Sir Stephen told Nathalie to take the loop of the leash and walk about the room. Three times Nathalie walked about the room; and O, naked and masked, drawn along on a leash attached to her belly, walked after the child. 'I suppose so,' said Sir Stephen. 'The Commander feels that every blade of hair ought to be removed. It looks as though he were right. You can attend to that tomorrow. For the time being, keep the chain on.'

That evening, for the first time in Jacqueline's and Nathalie's company, in René's and Sir Stephen's, O dined naked, her chain drawn back between her legs, up between her buttocks, and wrapped around her waist. Norah alone served the table, and O evaded her eyes.

It was the fresh, seeping lacerations even more than the irons and the brand on her buttocks which staggered the young lady at the Beauty Institute to which, the next day, O repaired to have herself plucked. It was in vain O told her that depilation by the wax method – consisting of pouring molten wax over

the skin and, when the wax has hardened, removing it and the
hair it has hardened upon – is quite as dreadful as a good
beating with a crop, in vain she repeated to her, and even en-
deavoured to explain, if not exactly what her fate had been, at
least that she considered herself happy in it; there was no way
of putting the young lady at her ease, she remained both scan-
dalized and terrified. O sought to soothe her, with the one
result that, instead of being looked on with pity, as she had
been at first, she ended up being regarded with horror. Gentle
as was the manner in which she thanked the young woman
when the job was completed and she was about to leave the
little cabinet where she had been spread out upon a table as
though for making love, considerable as was the sum of money
she paid and generous as was the tip she left, rather than feeling
that she was leaving the Beauty Institute, she had the feeling
that she was being expelled from it. Well, what did it matter?
It had been plain to her that there was indeed something
clashing in the contrast between the fur on her belly and the
feathers on her mask, and likewise plain that this Egyptian
statue aspect the mask conferred upon her, and which her broad
shoulders, her slender haunches and long legs emphasized, required that her flesh be perfectly smooth. But only effigies of
savage goddesses displayed so high and so visibly the cleft of
the sex between whose outer set of lips appeared the crest of
the finer inner set. And does one ever see statues or goddesses
wearing rings at their bellies? O recalled the plump red-haired
girl who had been at Anne-Marie's, and who had told her that
her master never used the ring at her belly except to fasten her
to the foot of his bed, and also that he liked her to be entirely
shaven, since only thus did she appear entirely naked. O feared
displeasing Sir Stephen who was so fond of drawing her to
him by her fleece, but she was wrong: if anything, Sir Stephen
found her more exciting, and when she had put her mask on
again, wiped away the lipstick from her mouth and the rouge
from the lips of her sex, and when those lips were so pale, he
caressed her in a manner that was almost timid, as one does an
animal one wishes to tame. As to the place to which he wished
to take her he had, so far, said nothing, nor anything about the

hour at which they would leave, nor who the Commander's guests would be. But he came to where she was and for the remainder of the afternoon slept beside her, and later had dinner brought to them in her room.

They left an hour before midnight, in the Buick, O swathed in a great brown huntsman's cape, and wearing moccasins on her feet; Nathalie was there too, she was wearing black trousers and sweater, holding O's leash whose leather loop was fastened to the bracelet the child wore on her right wrist; and Sir Stephen drove.

The moon, almost full, was high, was bright, shedding great snowy pools of light upon the road, the trees, the houses in the villages the road passed through, and leaving sunk in an India-ink blackness whatever it did not illumine. Night-time, and there were still a few groups of people or individual souls up, standing in doorways. And when this large closed car passed (Sir Stephen had not lowered the convertible top), one could sense curiosity stirring in the shadows. Dogs barked. On the side of the road the headlights lit, the olive-trees resembled silvery clouds drifting a man's height above the earth, the cypresses rose like the vanes of black feathers. There was nothing true nor real in this countryside which night made imaginary, nothing save the odour of sage and lavender. The road climbed and continued to climb, but it was the same warm wind that soughed over the earth. O slipped her cape off her shoulders. Ah, she'd not be seen, there wasn't anyone to see her, there wasn't anyone left. Ten minutes later, after having driven past a wood of holm-oaks lining one side of the road, Sir Stephen slowed the car, drove alongside a wall, slowed to a stop at the gate: it opened, they drove through. As the gate was being closed behind them, Sir Stephen parked, he got out, had Nathalie get out; he told O to leave her cape and moccasins in the car, and then to get out; she did. He opened a little gate. They found themselves in a little cloister with Renaissance arcades; of it, only three sides remained standing. The fourth-side of the flag-stoned courtyard extended into a terrace, also flagstoned. A dozen couples were dancing on the terrace and in the courtyard, some women in very low-cut

gowns and some men in white dinner jackets were sitting round
candlelit tables; the phonograph was in the gallery to the left, a
buffet table was set in the gallery to the right. But the moon
was shedding as much light as the candles, and when it fell full
upon O, whom Nathalie, a little black shadow, was pulling
ahead by the leash, those who caught sight of her stopped
dancing, and men got up from their chairs. The caterer in
charge of the phonograph, sensing something in the air, turned
around and, stunned, switched off the music. O had come to a
halt. Sir Stephen, also motionless, was waiting, two paces behind her. The Commander shouldered past those who had clustered around O and who had already brought improvised tor-
ches and candlesticks in order to see her better, and from closer
on. 'Who is it?' people were asking. 'To whom does she belong?'

'To you, if you like,' said the Commander, and he led
Nathalie and O towards a corner of the terrace where a stone
bench covered with cushions was set next to a little wall. When
O had sat down, her back pressed to the wall, her hands resting on her knees, and Nathalie had sat down on the ground at
her feet, the end of the chain still in her hand, the Commander faced the company. O searched the crowd, looking for Sir
Stephen. At first she did not see him. Then she sensed that he
was there, over there, further over, reclining in a deck-chair
at the other corner of the terrace. He could see her; she was
reassured. The music had started again, the dancers were dancing again. At first, one or two dancing couples steered towards her, as though accidentally, then moved on; then one of
the couples headed deliberately towards her, the woman guid-
ing the man. O stared at them through her plumage, stared at
them with wide-open eyes, eyes as round and as open as the
night bird she represented, and so strong was the illusion that
it struck everyone as completely natural that, when questioned,
this owl prove truly what it was, deaf to human speech and
mute. Between midnight and dawn, which was beginning to
pale away in the east, for the hour was approaching five, as the
moon grew ever paler people approached her, several people
did, came close enough to touch her, once formed a circle

around her, then formed another, several times opened her knees, raising the chain, then brought one of those double candlesticks of Provençal faïence – and she felt the candle-flames warm the inner sides of her thighs – to see just how that chain was attached; there was even a drunk American who, laughing loudly, put his hand to her belly but, upon realizing that he had taken hold of a handful of flesh and also of steel, he became suddenly sober and O saw the same horror and loathing appear on his face that she had earlier seen on the face of the young lady who had depilated her; he fled; and there was also a very young girl, bare-shouldered, wearing a tiny pearl choker, dressed in the kind of white dress that little girls put on when they go to their first ball, she had on gilded sandals and she was with a boy who made her sit down next to O. The boy took her hand and forced her to caress O's breasts, and O quivered under the cool hand; and then he made her touch O's sex, and the hole through which the ring passed; the little girl obeyed in silence, and when the boy said that, later on, he would have the same thing done to her, she listened quietly. But even though they did these things to O, used her thus, even taking her for an example, or for a sample, or for the object of a demonstration, not once did anyone address a word to her. Was she then a thing of stone or wax, or a creature of some other world, and was it that they thought it pointless to try to speak to her, or was it that they didn't dare? It was not until daybreak and after, when all the dancers had departed, that Sir Stephen and the Commander, rousing Nathalie, who was asleep at O's feet, had O get up, led her to the centre of the courtyard, detached her chain and took off her mask: and, laying her down upon a table, possessed her, now the one, now the other.

THE END

There existed another ending to the story of O. Seeing herself about to be left by Sir Stephen, she preferred to die. To which he gave his consent.

JEAN PAULHAN

A SLAVE'S REVOLT

An Essay on

The Story of O

In the course of the year 1838, an unusual rebellion bloodied the peaceful island of Barbadoes in the West Indies. Some two hundred Blacks, women as well as men and all of them promoted to freedom by the decrees promulgated in March of that year, one morning presented themselves at the door of their former master, a certain Glenelg, and besought him to take them back into bondage. In the name of the group, an Anabaptist minister had drawn up a list of grievances; they were read out to Glenelg and then the discussion began. But whether because of distrust, or scruples, or simple fear of the law, the former slaveowner refused to be convinced: whereupon he was, first of all, mildly pushed about, then, together with his family, massacred by the Blacks who that same evening went back to their cabins, their palaverings, their labours and all their accustomed activities. Governor MacGregor quickly took matters in hand, the affair was brought to a swift conclusion, and the Emancipation resumed its forward march. As for the little notebook in which the list of complaints was entered, it has never been recovered.

I sometimes think of that notebook. In all likelihood it included – apart from the most just charges relating to the organization of the workhouses, the substitution of the prison cell for the lash, and the prohibition forbidding the 'apprentices' (as the newly-freed labourers were called) to fall ill – at least the sketch of an apology for slavery. The remark, for example, that the only freedoms we really care about are those which directly cast others into an equivalent servitude. He is not a man who rejoices at being able to draw a breath of free air. Now if, for example, I obtain the right to play the banjo gaily until two o'clock in the morning, my neighbour loses the right not to hear me play the banjo until two o'clock in the morning. If I succeed in doing nothing, my neighbour must work not for one person, but for two. And, moreover, we know that an unconditional passion for freedom never fails, in this world, to bring on no less unconditional conflicts and wars in its wake. Add also that the slave being destined, according to the Dialectic, someday to become master in his turn, it should doubtless be a mistake to try to hurry the laws of nature. Add, finally, that there is a grandeur and there is a joy as well in abandoning oneself to the will of others (lovers and mystics are familiar with this sense of grandeur, this taste of joy) and in finding oneself, at last! rid of the weight of one's own pleasures, interests and personal complexes. In a word, that little notebook would, even more so today than a hundred and twenty years ago, have the flavour of heresy: of a dangerous book.

We are dealing here with another sort of dangerous books. With erotic ones, to be precise.

1. *Decisive as a letter.*

And indeed why call them dangerous? There is to say the least something imprudent in describing them thus. Thus described, they are endowed with something which quickens our desire to read them, which — and in these matters we usually show ourselves courageous — invites us to expose ourselves to peril. And it is not without reason geographical societies recommend that, when giving accounts of their travels, their members refrain from stressing the dangers they have encountered abroad: it is not a question of appearing modest, but rather of leading no one to temptation (wars, we discover from soldiers of fortune, are all too easily fought). But what dangers?

From where I am standing I have a clear view of at least one. It is a modest danger. By all evidence *The Story of O* is one of those books which mark the reader — which do not leave him entirely, or at all, such as he was before : one of those books whose meaning is curiously bound up with the influence they exert, which become transformed as that influence changes. Several years later they cease to be the same books; and it is not long before the critics who first appraised them are proven to have been great simpletons. But never mind. A critic should never hesitate, if need be, to adopt a ridiculous posture. Later, the easiest thing to say will be that, at the time, I rather lost my bearings, was at sea. I make a strange kind of progress as I advance in *The Story of O,* advancing as through a fairy-tale — fairy-tales, we know, are the erotic novels of children — advancing as though making my way through one of those fairy-tale castles which seems completely deserted even though the armchairs under their dust-covers and the tuffets and the four-poster beds look spick and span and the whips and scourges are in applepie order — if I may express myself thus, it is the very nature of all these things to be fresh and tidy. Not a suspicion of rust on the chains, not a spot on the windowpanes (multicoloured windowpanes). If there is any one word that comes to my mind when I think of *The Story of O,* it is *decency.* It might prove rather too difficult to justify that word; so let us continue. And that wind which blows unceasingly, sighing through all the rooms — there blows through *The Story of O* it is hard to determine just what kind of ghostly air, always pure and violent, always there, always unalloyed. It is a decisive, stubborn magical spirit : nothing halts or confounds it, nothing, whether moans or horrors, or ecstasy or nausea. And — if I must confess it again — my taste most often inclines in another direction : I prefer the work whose author paused, hesitated, the work in which, by some hint of awkwardness or doubt, he indicates that his subject intimidated him at first, that there was a moment when he was not sure he would be able to extricate himself from the difficulty. But from beginning to end, *The Story of O* is rather managed like a brilliant feat of arms. This has the look more of a speech or a lecture than of plain effusion; of a letter more than of a diary. But to whom is

163

the letter addressed? And whom does the discourse aim to convince? Whom is one to ask? I don't even know who you are.

I have very little doubt but that you are a woman. What makes me sure is not so much the details you delight in employing – green satin dresses, wasp-waist bodices, multiple petticoats, a ringlet of hair caught in a curler – as this: upon the same day René abandons her to further torments, O keeps her wits sufficiently about her to be able to observe that her lover's slippers have got scuffed and frayed, that a new pair must be bought for him. Such a thing, such a detail seems almost unimaginable to me – a man would never have fancied such a thing. Would not at any rate have dared mention it.

But all the same O gives expression, in her manner, to an ideal which is virile. Virile, or at least masculine. Here we have it at last: a woman who admits it! Admits what? Exactly what women have always – and never more so than today – forbidden themselves to admit. Exactly what men have always accusingly said was true about them: that they never cease slavishly to obey their blood and temper; that, in them, everything, even their minds, even their souls, is dominated by their sex. That they have got incessantly to be fed, incessantly washed and burdened, incessantly beaten. That they have but one requirement, and that is simply of a good master who takes good care to keep his goodness in check and to be wary of it: for it will be to make themselves loved by others that they will put to use all the high-spiritedness, the joy, the gay disposition which becomes theirs as a result of our tenderness towards them when once we declare our tender feelings. That, in a word, one must have a whip in hand when one goes to visit them. Few are the men who have not dreamt of possessing a Justine. But as best I know no woman has so far dreamt of being Justine. At any rate dreamt it aloud, and into her yearning put this pride in grief and tears, this conquering violence, this rapacious eagerness to suffer, this will to suffer keyed to the bursting point. A woman you may be, but one about whom there is something of the knight, the crusader. It is as if you were twin-natured, or as if the person for whom the letter is intended were at every moment so near, so present that you

164

borrowed his tastes, assumed his voice. But what kind of a woman and who are you?

The Story of O seems to have come somehow from afar: I mean that in it I have a feeling of that restfulness and that spaciousness one finds in a story its author has carried within him for a long period – a story wherewith he has become familiar. Who is Pauline Réage? A dreamer and no more? – and there are such persons: it suffices, they say, to heed one's heart. It is a heart nothing is able to stop throbbing, living. Or is this a lady of wide experience who has dwelt a time in this strange world? Who has undergone these experiences and who is surprised to discover an adventure which began so promisingly – or at least so soberly: in self-abnegation and chastisement – finally turn out so badly and end upon a note of somewhat dubious satisfaction; for O lives in a kind of brothel into which she was led by love; there she stays and there as a matter of fact she gets along rather nicely. However, in this connection:

2. *A pitiless decency.*

I too am surprised by this ending. You will not be able to get the idea out of my head that it is not the true conclusion. That in reality (so to speak) your heroine succeeds in getting Sir Stephen to bring about her death. He'll not release her from bondage until once she is dead. Evidently, the last word has not been spoken, and this bee – I refer to Pauline Réage – has reserved some of the honey for herself. Who knows? perhaps upon this one occasion she was susceptible of the kind of consideration a writer would be subject to: at some later time to write the sequel to O's adventures. Or on the other hand that ending is so self-evident it wasn't worth the bother to describe; we'll find it out by ourselves and without the least effort. We shall find it out . . . and it rather obsesses us. But as for yourself, how did you invent it and what is the clue that explains this tale? My thoughts hark back to this, so sure am I that, when found, the tuffets and the four-posters and the chains will be explained too, will allow to move back and forth through their midst that tall obscure figure, that phantom which gives their intention to these strange breaths of stirring air.

I must indeed at this point consider what there is in desire that is strange, alien, all but unbearable. One is made to think of those stones upon which the strong winds blow – stones which suddenly stir or begin to emit sighs, to give out the sounds of a mandolin being played. People come from great distances to see these things. But one's first impulse is to run away, however much one may be fond of music. And after all what if the role of erotic books (dangerous books, if you prefer) were to explain desire to us, to give us assurances, comfort us the way a confessor comforts? I know well enough that in general one becomes habituated to desire. And men don't find it an embarrassment for long. They make the best of it, resign themselves, say that after all it was they themselves who got the whole thing started. They lie and they lie in the face of the facts: the facts are there, evident. Only too evident.

Women lie too, someone will point out. To be sure, but with them the event is not visible. They can always say no. What decency! Whence doubtless comes the opinion that women are the more beautiful, that beauty is feminine. More beautiful? – I'm not sure. But more discreet – yes, more discreet, less transparent: there is something of beauty in that. And that is the second time I am put in mind of decency, all the while thinking of a book in which the question of decency figures very little.

But is it true that the question of decency is absent from *The Story of O*? I am not thinking now of the decency, a little dull and a little false, which is content to hide itself, which flees from before the stone and denies having seen it budge. There is another sort of decency, invincible and quick to punish, a decency which very sharply humiliates the flesh in order to return it to its former integrity, which forcefully sends it back to the days when desire was as yet undeclared in it and the rock had not yet sung: a decency into whose grip it is dangerous to fall. For it will be satisfied with nothing less than hands bound behind the back, unstrung knees, bodies drawn and quartered, both sweat and tears.

I seem to be saying frightful things. Perhaps, but if so, then that is because fear is our daily pittance – and dangerous books, it may be, are simply those which turn us over as captives to our natural danger. What lover would not be terrified were he for a single instant to gauge the portent and implications of the oath he swears, and swears by no means in an off-hand way, to be bound by his love for the rest of his life? And what mistress, if for a second she were to weigh the meaning of the 'before you came I knew nothing of love . . . never before we met did love stir me' which rise to her lips? Or again, and more prudently this time – prudently? –: 'I should like to punish myself for having been happy before I met you.' And there she is, trapped by her own words. There she is, done for, used.

And so there are tortures a-plenty in *The Story of O*. There are cuts from the riding-crop, branding with a red-hot iron to say nothing of the iron collar and the exposure in the middle of the terrace – almost as many tortures as there are prayers in the life of ascetics who inhabit the desert. Nor are they less carefully distinguished and virtually enumerated – one set off from the other by little stone markers. They are not always joyful tortures – I mean to say joyfully inflicted. René refuses to inflict them; and if Sir Stephen consents, it is as though he were performing a duty. From all evidence, the torturers do not find their work amusing. They have nothing of the sadistic in them. Everything happens as if from the outset it were O alone who demanded to be hurt, flushed from her retreat by punishment.

At this point some fool is probably going to raise the hue and cry of masochism. That is all very well with me: it is simply to add to the true mystery a false one compounded of pure language. What does *masochism* mean? That the pain *exists* at the same time as the pleasure does; and suffering at the same time as joy? That may be. These are some of those affirmations metaphysicians use a great deal – just as they say that any presence is an absence; every speech a silence – and I do not for one moment deny that (although I do not always understand them) they may have their meaning, or at the very least their usefulness. But it is a usefulness which, at any rate, is not apparent to ordinary observation – which, hence, is not the concern of the doctor, nor of the ordinary psychologist, nor, for all the more reason, of the everyday fool. 'No,' I hear someone reply. 'It is indeed a question of a pain, but of a pain the masochist knows how to *transform* into pleasure – of a suffering from which, by some alchemy whose secret he knows, he is able to extract an unalloyed joy.'

What tidings are there! And so it is thus man has finally discovered what for so long and so assiduously he has sought after in medicine, in ethics, in philosophies and in religions: the means to avoid pain – or more or less to overcome it: to understand it (whether by seeing in it the effect of our stupidity or of our mistakes). What is more, he might have happened upon the answer at almost any time in the past, for, after all, the masochists trace their ancestry back beyond yesterday. And I am astonished that the discovery did not result in the greatest honours being heaped upon those masochists, astonished that no attempts were made to glean their secret, that they were not collected together and fetched to palaces where they might the better have been observed in cages.

Perhaps men never ask themselves questions which have not already been answered. Perhaps it would be enough to put them in contact with each other, to snatch them from their solitude. Very well, here is the cage, and now here we have this young woman inside the cage. All one has to do now is listen to her.

3. *Curious love-letter*.

She says: You have no sound cause to be surprised. Look more closely at your love. It would be terrified if it were to understand for an instant that I am a woman, and alive. And it is not by forgetting the fiery wells from which the blood rises that you are going to dry them up.

'Your jealousy does not deceive me. True, you make me happy and healthy and a thousand times more alive. However, there is nothing I can do to prevent this happiness of mine from turning immediately against you. The stone also sings the more loudly when the blood is easy and the body at rest. Rather keep me confined in this cage and give me sparingly to eat, if you dare. Everything whereby I am brought nearer to illness and to death renders me more faithful. And it is only then, during those moments when you make me suffer, that I am out of danger. You should not accept to be a god unto me if the gods' duties frighten you, and everyone knows that the gods are not so kind, not so tender. You have now got to acquire a taste for my tears. Come now; is not my neck charming when, despite all I can do, my throat fills and trembles with a cry I strive to repress? Nothing is truer: you must have a whip with you when you come to see us. And better still, more than one; you must bring a cat-o'-nine-tails.'

And she says at once: 'What kind of a joke in what kind of bad taste? Eh, but you understand nothing. And if I were not wildly in love with you, do you suppose I would dare to speak to you in this way? and to betray my own tastes?'

She adds: 'My imagination, my vague dreams – they betray you endlessly. Weary me, exhaust me. Rid me of those dreams. Deliver me. Take the lead, make haste so that I shall not even have the time to *dream* that I am unfaithful to you. (The reality preoccupies me less.) But take care first to mark me with your emblem. If I bear traces of your lash or of your chains, or if I keep these rings through my lips, then it will be plain to everyone that I belong to you. As long as I am beaten, everywhere violated, I am naught but the thought of you, desire of you, obsession of you. You wanted that, didn't you? I think you did. Well, I love you, and that is also what I want.

'If once and for all I cease to be my own, if my mouth and my belly and my breasts belong to me no longer, I shall become the creature of another world where the meaning of everything has been changed. One day, perhaps, I shall know nothing about myself anymore. And then what will they mean to me, what effect will they be able to have upon me, the pleasure and the caresses of so many men – your envoys, I cannot discern, cannot see, cannot compare with you?'

That is what she says and in that manner. I listen to her and clearly recognize that she is not lying. I strive to follow her (it is her prostitution which has confused and troubled me for a long time). Perhaps, after all, the flesh-devouring robe of the myths is more than mere allegory, and sacred whoredom something other than an historical curiosity. It may be that the bonds and chains in naive songs and the 'I die for love of thee' are not simple metaphors, nor, likewise, what street-walkers declare to their true loves: 'I've got you under my skin, do with me whatever you wish.' (It is odd that in order to get rid of a feeling or sentiment which baffles us we adopt the expedient of ascribing it to wild Indians or to prostitutes.) It may be that in writing to Abelard: 'I shall be thy whore' Heloise did not simply wish to turn a pretty phrase. *The Story of O* is surely the most fiercely intense love-letter a man could ever receive.

I am reminded of that Dutchman doomed forever to fly upon the face of the oceans until that time when he shall find a girl willing to give up her life to save him; and of the knight Guiguemar who, that his wounds may be mended, awaits a woman who will suffer for him 'what ere this never hath woman suffered.' Indeed, O's story is longer than a lay or a legend and far more detailed than an ordinary letter; perhaps it was necessary for her to go back a long time. Perhaps it has never been more difficult than it is today to understand what the boys and girls in the street are saying – what, I suppose, the slaves of Barbadoes said a century ago. We are living in a time when the simplest truths have no course but to come back to us naked (as O is naked) and wearing a mask of old wisdom.

For these days you hear normal-looking people, and even very sensible people, who are pleased to talk about love as about a light sensation without much importance. It promises a good deal of pleasure, they say, and the contact between one epidermis and another is something not entirely lacking in charm. They go on to say that the charm or the pleasure operate with maximum effect upon him who manages to keep his fantasy, his caprice and nothing more or less than his natural freedom from becoming entangled in an affair of love. I have no objections to raise to this, and if it is so exceedingly easy for persons of different sex (or mayhap of the same) to give each other joy, they are doing wonderfully well and would be very mistaken to do otherwise. In all that there are only one or two words which trouble me: the word *love* and also the word *freedom*. It goes without saying, and by definition, that it is all quite the contrary. Love? That is when one depends — and depends, not only in one's pleasure-taking, but in one's very existence, and in what comes before existence: in the desire one has to exist — upon fifty curious things: upon two lips (and upon the pout or the smile they compose), upon a shoulder (upon that particular way it has of lifting or falling), upon two eyes (upon a glance that seems ever so much more inviting, or faintly more forbidding), in a word, upon the entirety of a foreign body together with the spirit or the soul that there is in it — upon a body which at any moment may become more able to dazzle than the sun, more chilling than a wilderness of snow and ice. Tortures? Your tortures make me laugh; I tell you that to love is no joke. One trembles when that body stoops to fasten the strap upon a little shoe, and it seems as though everyone were watching you tremble. Rather the whip, better rings passed through the flesh. As for freedom . . . No matter what man, or what woman, having once been through this will sooner be moved to cry out against freedom, to burst forth with curses and abominations damning freedom. No, horrors are not wanting in the story O tells. But it sometimes seems to me that, instead of a young woman, it is an idea, a mode of ideas, an opinion which in this book finds itself put to the torture.

The truth about the revolt.

Strange, but nowadays the idea of happiness in bondage has the look of something novel. Little is left in families of the law that gave the father the power of life or death over his children, nor in schools of corporal punishment or bullying, nor in households of wife-beating, and the same men past ages boldly beheaded on the public square now are left sadly to

171

pine away and rot in cellars. The only tortures we inflict are anonymous and unmerited. And upon that account they are a thousand times more atrocious: it is a city's whole population which all at one stroke is roasted over a grill in wartime. The father's excessive kindness, the teacher's, or the lover's is compensated for by air-strikes, by deluges of napalm and the explosion of atoms. Everything moves along as if in the world there existed a certain mysterious equilibrium of violence for which we have lost the taste and of which we have forgotten the meaning. And I am by no means sorry that it is a woman who has recaptured them again. No, I am not even surprised.

To tell the truth, I am surprised there are any (any women). More than surprised: vaguely wonderstruck. Whence, perhaps, the reason they seem wonderful to me; whence the fact I seldom cease longing for them. What is it exactly that I long for?

It happens sometimes that I regret my childhood. But it is not by any means the surprises and the revelations poets speak of that I regret. No, memories of childhood bring back to me a time when I was responsible for the whole world. Now a boxing champion or a cook, now a politician (yes), now a general, a thief and even a Redskin, a tree, a rock. It was a game, was it? Yes, very much of a game for you, you grown-ups, but no game for me, not at all. I had the world in the palm of my hand in those days, the world and also the cares and the dangers which go with it: I was universal in those days. This is what I am driving at.

To women at least it is given to resemble, all their life long, the children we used once to be. A woman knows all about a thousand things which are beyond me. Generally, she knows about sewing. She can cook. She knows how an apartment ought to be arranged and which styles don't clash (I am not saying she can do all that to perfection, but neither, for my part, was I an irreproachable Redskin). And she knows a lot more: she gets on easily with cats and dogs; she is able to converse with those half-lunatic creatures – children – we let into the house. She teaches them about the stars and the skies and good manners and hygiene, teaches them fairy-tales, and things can even go as far as the piano. In short, from childhood on we

172

never stop dreaming of a man who would be every kind of man rolled into one; but it appears as if it is granted to each woman to be all women (and all men) at the same time. And that's not all.

These days you hear them say that one has only to understand everything in order to forgive anything. Well, it has always seemed to me that for women — so universal are they — it was just the other way around. I had a good number of friends who took me for what I was, and in my turn I took them for what they were — they had not the slightest desire to change me, nor I them. And I even used to be glad — and they used to be glad too — that each one of us was so much like his own self. But there is not a single woman who does not attempt to change the man she loves, and to change herself as she does so. As if the proverb lied — as if one had but to understand everything in order to forgive nothing at all.

No, Pauline Réage does not forgive herself much. And I even wonder, when all is said and done, whether she doesn't exaggerate somewhat: whether her fellow-women are indeed so much alike as she supposes. But that is what more than one man would all too willingly grant her.

Must one regret the Barbadoes slaves' catalogue of grievances? To tell the truth, I fear that the worthy Anabaptist who drew it up may have cluttered it, in the part given over to apologetics, with pretty dull commonplaces: for example, that there will always be slaves (that, at any rate, is thoroughly evident); that they will always be the same (that may be subject to doubt); that one must resign oneself to one's sort and state and not waste in recriminations a time which could otherwise be spent in playing games, in meditating, in the usual pleasures. And so on. But I have an idea that he omitted to mention the truth: that Glenelg's slaves loved their master; that they could not do without him. The same truth, after all, from which *The Story of O* derives its decisiveness, its incredible decency and that strong fanatical wind that blows through it without pausing once.

THE END

VALLEY OF THE DOLLS BY JACQUELINE SUSANN

Valley of the Dolls is about the world where sex is a success weapon, where love is the smiling mask of hate, where slipping youth and fading beauty are ever-present spectres. It is a world where the magic tickets to peace or oblivion are 'dolls' – the insider's word for pills – pep pills, sleeping pills, red pills, blue pills ... and pills to chase the truth away.

Valley of the Dolls is the story of three of the most exciting women you'll ever meet; women who were too tough or too talented not to reach the top ... and unable to enjoy it once they were there!

Valley of the Dolls is the all-time bestseller you can't afford to miss!

0 552 07807 7   £1.75

From the author of the world best-selling *Valley of the Dolls* – JACQUELINE SUSANN –

THE LOVE MACHINE

is the story of Robin Stone – a brilliant, ruthless man – and of three women who love him. It is a story set against the background of the tough, superheated world of show business and big-time television – the world Robin Stone has set out to conquer.

His conquest takes him into the arena of big money and big power. But beneath the surface of success, of expensive restaurants, penthouse offices, private airplanes and lavish living, lies the world the public never learns about – a world of uninhibited orgies in London, of 'gay' parties in Hollywood, of sordid deals in which love and sex are coldly bartered.

In this hidden world, seeking to satisfy longings he cannot admit to himself, Robin Stone is driven from those who love him and whose love he cannot accept to a series of harrowing experiences and – ultimately – to the agonized discovery of the truth about himself and his past ...

0 552 08523 5   £1.75

PORTNOY'S COMPLAINT BY PHILIP ROTH

PORTNOY'S COMPLAINT – a disorder in which strongly felt ethical and altruistic impulses are perpetually warring with extreme longings, often of a perverse nature. Alexander Portnoy is 33 years old, a bachelor, the Assistant Commissioner for the City of New York Commission on Human Opportunity, and a Jew . . .

The book is written in the manner of a confession to his psychiatrist, and Portnoy says: 'This is my life, and I'm living it in the middle of a Jewish joke. I am the son in the Jewish joke – ONLY IT AIN'T NO JOKE!'

'A deliciously funny book, absurd and exuberant, wild and uproarious.' – *New York Times*

0 552 11614 9   £1.50

GOODBYE COLUMBUS BY PHILIP ROTH

'The first time I saw Brenda she asked me to hold her glasses.'

From this innocuous beginning, Neil – a college boy – and Brenda, the pampered daughter of a wealthy manufacturer, spent a long summer celebrating their new-found love. They spent the hot days teasing and tantalising each other, and the hot nights making love.

Included with this story, which won its author, Philip Roth, the coveted National Book Award, are five of his short stories: THE CONVERSION OF THE JEWS, DEFENDER OF THE FAITH, EPSTEIN, YOU CAN'T TELL A MAN BY THE SONG HE SINGS, and ELI THE FANATIC.

GOODBYE COLUMBUS was also made into a highly successful film, starring Richard Benjamin and Ali MacGraw.

0 552 10976 2   85p

A SELECTED LIST OF FINE FICTION PUBLISHED BY CORGI

WHILE EVERY EFFORT IS MADE TO KEEP PRICES LOW, IT IS SOME-TIMES NECESSARY TO INCREASE PRICES AT SHORT NOTICE. CORGI BOOKS RESERVE THE RIGHT TO SHOW AND CHARGE NEW RETAIL PRICES ON COVERS WHICH MAY DIFFER FROM THOSE ADVERTISED IN THE TEXT OR ELSEWHERE.

THE PRICES SHOWN BELOW WERE CORRECT AT THE TIME OF GOING TO PRESS (DECEMBER '80).

All these books are available at your bookshop or newsagent ; or can be ordered direct from the publisher. Just tick the titles you want and fill in the form below.

CORGI BOOKS, Cash Sales Department, P.O. Box 11, Falmouth, Cornwall.

Please send cheque or postal order, no currency.

U.K. Please allow 30p for the first book, 15p for the second book and 12p for each additional book ordered to a maximum charge of £1.29.

B.F.P.O. and Eire allow 30p for the first book, 15p for the second book plus 12p per copy for the next 7 books, thereafter 6p per book.

Overseas customers. Please allow 50p for the first book plus 15p per copy for each additional book.

NAME (block letters) ....

ADDRESS ....

(DEC. 1980) ....